Jackson's wolf was going crazy at the thought of Harris wearing his things. Sweat trickled down his back, and his body felt tender and hot, like the shift was prickling at his skin. It had never been like this with Raoul or his other boyfriends. He had no idea what was going on or why it was directed at one of his best friends. A mix of anxiety and homesickness, perhaps, and all of it focused on Harris because he was always such a comforting, solid presence.

Jackson snorted. That was all bullshit. He had a good old-fashioned crush, and he couldn't explain it away as his worry over the new job.

No, this was carnal lust mixed with affection. Dammit.

It was ridiculous. They'd been friends for over a decade. He wouldn't throw away their friendship for a fuck. Harris was worth more than that.

God, he was such a dick.

WELCOME TO

Dear Reader,

Everyone knows love brings a touch of magic to your life. And the presence of paranormal thrills can make a romance that much more exciting. Dreamspun Beyond selections tell stories of love featuring your favorite shifters, vampires, wizards, and more falling in love amid paranormal twists. Stories that make your breath catch and your imagination soar.

In the pages of these imaginative love stories, readers can escape to a contemporary world flavored with a touch of the paranormal where love conquers all despite challenges, the thrill of a first kiss sweeps you away, and your heart pounds at the sight of the one you love. When you put it all together, you discover romance in its truest form, no matter what world you come from.

Love sees no difference.

Elizabeth North

Executive Director
Dreamspinner Press

Bru Baker

Hiding In Plain Sight

Published by

Published by
DREAMSPINNER PRESS

5032 Capital Circle SW, Suite 2, PMB# 279,
Tallahassee, FL 32305-7886 USA
www.dreamspinnerpress.com

This is a work of fiction. Names, characters, places, and incidents either are the product of author imagination or are used fictitiously, and any resemblance to actual persons, living or dead, business establishments, events, or locales is entirely coincidental.

Hiding In Plain Sight
© 2018 Bru Baker.
Editorial Development by Sue Brown-Moore.

Cover Art
© 2018 Aaron Anderson.
aaronbydesign55@gmail.com
Cover content is for illustrative purposes only and any person depicted on the cover is a model.

Paperback ISBN: 978-1-64108-108-5
Digital ISBN: 978-1-64080-866-9
Library of Congress Control Number: 2018941318
Paperback published September 2018
v. 1.0

Printed in the United States of America
∞
This paper meets the requirements of
ANSI/NISO Z39.48-1992 (Permanence of Paper).

BRU BAKER got her first taste of life as a writer at the tender age of four, when she started publishing a weekly newspaper for her family. What they called nosiness she called a nose for news, and no one was surprised when she ended up with degrees in journalism and political science and started a career in journalism.

Bru spend more than a decade writing for newspapers before making the jump to fiction. She now works in reference and readers' advisory in a Midwestern library, though she still finds it hard to believe someone's willing to pay her to talk about books all day. Most evenings you can find her curled up with a book or her laptop. Whether it's creating her own characters or getting caught up in someone else's, there's no denying that Bru is happiest when she's engrossed in a story. She and her husband have two children, which means a lot of her books get written from the sidelines of various sports practices.

Website: www.bru-baker.com

Blog: www.bru-baker.blogspot.com

Twitter: @bru_baker

Facebook: www.facebook.com/bru.baker79

Goodreads: www.goodreads.com/author/show/6608093.Bru_Baker

Email: bru@bru-baker.com

By Bru Baker

DREAMSPUN BEYOND
CAMP H.O.W.L.
#7 – Camp H.O.W.L.
#22 – Under a Blue Moon
#28 – Hiding In Plain Sight

DREAMSPUN DESIRES
#31 – Tall, Dark, and Deported

Published by **DREAMSPINNER PRESS**
www.dreamspinnerpress.com

For Kristin, Caraway, Hunter, Ruth, and everyone else
who answers when I ask,
"Do you think werewolves can…?"
Thanks for feeding the creative fires!

Chapter One

HARRIS groaned when his alarm went off, rolling over and slapping his palm over the snooze button for five more precious minutes of sleep. He buried his head under his pillow to block out the light and cursed Anne Marie for calling an emergency staff meeting at 8:00 a.m. on the only Saturday he had off all month.

He'd planned to sleep in, indulge in a little self-love, and spend the day binge-watching shows. Tomorrow he had plans to make the long drive to Lexington to spend the day with Jackson and Jordan. There was a Korean barbecue place with killer kalbi he'd been craving for weeks. It was a little mom-and-pop place that seated ten, tops. The atmosphere was a lot like his grandmother's kitchen in San Francisco, where he'd learned to make crispy lumpia and other dishes she said were important because they reminded the family of their history.

There weren't any Filipino restaurants in the Midwest, but he'd learned to take what he could get. The Korean place was in a seedy neighborhood, but everyone respected the owners enough not to cause any trouble for them. Besides, only an idiot would try to mug a werewolf. Harris was packed with lean muscle, but he was scrawny for a Were. Jackson and Jordan were both stacked because of their jobs. Even without letting the werewolf secret out of the bag, they radiated danger.

Maybe he'd try to convince Jackson to wear his police uniform. Just for safety's sake. The sight of him in his uniform never failed to make Harris's palms go sweaty and his heart race.

Harris snorted and burrowed farther under the pillow. Jackson in uniform was a favorite jerk-off fantasy for him, but he didn't have time for that right now. He needed to get his happy ass to the staff meeting. Anne Marie wasn't above sending a search party if someone was late, and Drew and Nick would burst right into his bedroom no matter what he was doing. Assholes.

He got up with a growl and turned off the alarm, proud of himself for not taking the whole five minutes to sulk. He ran a hand over his barely there stubble and decided it could go another day as he stumbled into the bathroom to get ready. Even without a shave, he'd be cutting it close, but he wasn't willing to forgo a shower. It was just common decency when you lived with a bunch of werewolves.

By the time he'd showered and changed, it was five till, so there was no chance of grabbing breakfast. Luckily Drew always kept food stocked in the infirmary kitchen, including Harris's favorite tea.

It was ten past by the time he ambled onto the infirmary's porch, sipping his ginger tea. He raised a brow when he saw only Scott and Kaylee.

Harris settled into a rocking chair. It didn't look like the other two had been there long. They were alone on the porch, though he heard heartbeats upstairs, so he knew Drew and Nick were there. Probably grabbing a quickie. Bastards.

He was glad they'd finally gotten their heads out of their asses and admitted they were gone for each other. He was. But now he'd had a full year of them stinking up every room with their hormones and making googly eyes at each other. Not to mention coming to every staff meeting reeking of sex. Maybe they should find a new place for staff meetings. Drew's screened-in porch was outfitted with comfortable furniture and large enough to hold all the Camp H.O.W.L. staff, but there were more important things than physical comfort—like the assurance that no one would be walking in on them having sex. Drew was a great guy, but he was also Jackson's little brother. He would entertain zero fantasies of Drew.

"Where is everyone, anyway? I thought the queen bee said eight."

"There's a huge food fight in the mess," Kaylee said with a grin.

God. They happened every few months. It was a natural hazard when dealing with teenagers, especially teenagers who had super strength and the ability to shift into wolves. Their adrenaline and stress needed an outlet, which was why the staff worked so hard to keep them busy. But every so often a group cropped up that was… extra. Extra rowdy, extra loud, extra stupid. This was one of those groups.

"Great day to be alive, isn't it?" Scott asked, wrapping his arm around Kaylee.

She snorted and pushed him away. "Great day to have off, you mean."

"Same thing."

Harris grinned. They'd all three be in the mess at ground zero if it wasn't their weekend off. The knowledge that everyone else was having a terrible day tempered his annoyance at having to get up so early.

Scott gave Kaylee a noogie and yelped when she bit him. "We're going into Bloomington to see a movie and get dinner and drinks later. You wanna come?"

Harris wondered if the two of them would stop pulling each other's pigtails long enough to watch a movie. Unlikely. Odds were good they'd be kicked out of the theater.

"As enticing as that isn't," he said, earning a laugh from Kaylee and an indignant sound from Scott, "I've got a date with Netflix."

"Come with us," Scott said. "Friends don't let friends waste their weekend off holed up watching Bruce Willis movies."

"I'm not watching Bruce Willis movies," Harris snapped. "Besides, I'm not wasting anything. I'm going to Lexington tomorrow for the day."

"Ooh," Kaylee chimed in. "Gonna get some?"

He wished. "No, I'm going to go see Jackson and Jordan. It's been a few weeks, and they want to catch up."

It had been over four weeks, but who was counting? Having Drew here at camp meant he was seeing a lot more of Jackson than usual. But things at the station had been busier than normal, so Jackson missed the last monthly dinner.

Scott laughed and elbowed Kaylee in the ribs. "That sounds good. Wanna 'catch up' later, Kaylee?"

She punched him hard in the thigh, but from the look on her face, some catching up was definitely in the cards. Gross.

Harris ignored them and sipped his tea, watching birds flit around the feeders near the pond outside. He'd still rather be sleeping, but it wasn't a bad way to spend the morning.

He scented Drew before he saw him, his nose wrinkling. As he'd predicted, Drew smelled like he'd rolled around in Nick's scent before coming down. Hell, Harris bet he had. They were newly mated—he didn't care what bullshit Pack law said about humans and Weres not mating; they *were* mated, not just married—and Nick had been aggressively scenting him since the wedding.

Harris didn't begrudge them their happiness at all. Finding a mate was a huge deal in Were culture. Harris didn't know what a fulfilled mate bond felt like, but he often wondered if it was as euphoric as it seemed. Mates were so connected and in tune with each other. He'd do anything to have that with his own mate, but their incomplete bond meant he was empty—there was nothing to pick up on besides his own longing and loneliness. That was hard to deal with, but Harris had been best friends with his mate for years before the mate bond formed. Jackson had always made it clear he wasn't interested in settling down, so when Harris realized he'd bonded with him, he'd kept it quiet. Friendship was all he could have with Jackson, and Harris would rather have that than nothing. Unrequited bonds were hard, but rejected ones were a million times worse.

"I was all prepared to make up excuses for being late, but I guess I'm in the clear," Drew said as he sat in the rocking chair next to Harris's.

A few moments later Nick appeared in the doorway with two steaming cups of coffee. He handed one to Drew and stole a kiss before sitting down on the wicker couch a few feet away.

Apparently, his inner wolf was satisfied by the way he'd painted Drew in his scent earlier, which was fortunate. They'd spent more than one staff meeting with Drew sitting in Nick's lap.

"Food fight in the mess," Harris explained.

Drew's eyes lit up. "Excellent!" He held up his coffee cup and clinked it against Harris's mug. "Cheers."

"Hallelujah. Praise be to days off," Nick muttered after a sip of his own coffee. "I had syrup in my hair for *days* after the last one."

Drew's scent took a cloying turn after that announcement, and Harris hurried to take his mind off whatever memory it had sparked.

"You two staying here today or heading off campus?"

Drew blinked and smiled. "We're going to Indianapolis. There's a driving range Nick wants to try, and I want to visit a few medical supply stores to see if I can do better than the place I'm ordering things from for the clinic."

"Romantic," Harris said.

"I know my man," Nick said, fluttering his eyelashes. "The best way to woo him is a good selection of stethoscopes and an unlimited supply of gauze."

Everyone except Drew turned at the sound of a group approaching. Anne Marie and the rest of the staff had arrived. That or the campers had won the food fight, and they were coming for them.

The whole group was chattering as they filed in, and they all looked pissed. Richard had a smear of butter on his forehead, and Stacy had an entire piece of bacon stuck in her dark curls. Even Kenya hadn't been spared; she had what looked like blueberry muffin stains all down her shirt. Everyone looked the worse for wear, and soon the porch smelled like brunch.

Anne Marie brought up the rear, ketchup and eggs smeared on her shirt. She had a fierce temper, and Harris didn't envy those kids. She was a take-no-prisoners kind of person when she was this angry. No doubt Alphas would be called and tears would be shed later this afternoon, none of them Anne Marie's.

"I have an addition to our roster for the next moon," she said without preamble. She handed Kaylee a stack of folders to pass out. "She's a high-profile wolfling, so we'll have to be extra vigilant about keeping a low profile while she's here. That means spot checks of campers' phones and disabling the Wi-Fi during lights-out hours. Her parents wanted us to install a cell blocking device, but I'm not comfortable with wolflings being separated from their parents and Packs without reason, so I said no. It's an option if things go badly after she arrives, though, and one I will consider if need be."

They normally had more warning about high-profile campers. "Why are we just hearing about this now?"

Anne Marie scowled at him. "Because *I* heard about it yesterday. There's a significant risk of exposure with this one, and her people are playing this close to their chests."

Harris took the folder Kaylee gave him and cracked it open. It was an intake profile like they got for all wolflings. He didn't recognize the name or the photo of the girl that accompanied it.

Anne Marie slapped a glossy magazine against his chest. By the time he looked at the cover, she was halfway across the room distributing more.

"I might be gay, but that doesn't mean I'm into trashy magazines," Harris said, scowling a bit at the girl on the cover, who was clad in a latex, bubblegum-pink pantsuit that left nothing to the imagination.

"Look closer, genius," Kaylee taunted. She was already flipping through her magazine, which looked like a different flavor of awful gossip rag than his.

Harris inspected the cover, his eyes roving over the headlines and little picture insets, until something in the cover model's eyes made him do a double take. He pulled out the intake form for comparison. Great. Their new wolfling was "America's Favorite Good Girl," according to the headline. *That* was what a good girl looked like? What the hell would they photograph a bad girl in? Pasties and a smile?

"That's right, folks. Kandie Bates is our newest Turn. Her given name is Candice Bachman, and if any of you leak that, your life won't be worth living. This girl is a scared wolfling worried about her Turn and managing her shift. She is not Kandie when she's here. Our high-profile camper protocol is in effect starting the moment campers arrive. You will watch your campers like hawks. No autograph requests, absolutely *no* photos, and no one, wolfling or staff, will breathe a word about her being here. Got it?"

Richard snorted. "You've got to be kidding me. A pop star?"

Anne Marie whipped around and glared him into silence. "First and foremost, she's a wolfling, Richard. It's our duty to help her through her Turn."

"Still—"

Kaylee cut him off. "And she's an actress, not a singer. If you're going to be a raging asshole, at least get it right."

"No one will be an asshole," Anne Marie said before Richard could respond. She only raised her voice a bit, but it was enough to send the entire porch into silence.

"Now, as I was saying, it is vitally important that we stick to our high-profile camper protocol. I don't need to tell you how disastrous it could be if word got out that she was here."

"What about when she gets back to Hollywood?" Richard asked, a vein popping in his forehead. "What safeguards do we have then?"

Anne Marie opened her binder. "On to the logistics," she said, ignoring Richard entirely. "Let's talk housing."

Harris pitied the poor soul who had her in their cabin. It would probably be Kaylee. She was a woman, after all. Not that they segregated the wolflings by sex in cabins. But she could relate or some shit. She'd taken Nick's cabin when he and Drew had gotten mated, freeing Nick up to move to the infirmary.

"Now, since Candice has privacy needs that are different from most of our campers, she'll be taking the guest room at the infirmary instead of sleeping in a cabin to start. If she feels comfortable, she'll move into Kaylee's cabin."

Harris breathed a sigh of relief, but a moment later Anne Marie pinned him with her bright blue gaze, and his heart sank.

"Harris, since she's specified she's more comfortable with a male therapist and you're the ranking dude, she's on your caseload for therapy."

Wonderful. He held back a groan since voicing his displeasure would only get him in trouble. With Anne Marie that might mean a reprimand or a smack to the head. Neither sounded like a great way to start his day off, so he kept mum.

"You'll also be the one to go get her from the airport," Anne Marie continued, and Harris couldn't hold back his outraged squawk at that news.

"Are you kidding me? If she's so rich and famous, she should be able to hire a car," he protested.

Usually campers arrived with parents, who would rent a car for the drive or hire cars to bring them to a hotel nestled in the Hoosier National Forest. They'd spend the night, and then someone, usually the groundskeeper, George, would fetch them the next morning and bring them to camp. It didn't bode well for her stay if this little starlet was already demanding special treatment.

"She could," Anne Marie said, the glint in her eye making Harris's balls draw up. "And she'd be recognized by the driver and the guests at the hotel. What part of low profile was unclear, Harris? You will be waiting there when her chartered plane lands, and you will drive her straight back to camp, no stops. Got it?"

Harris swallowed. He hadn't thought about the potential for exposure. "Got it."

"Good. Her flight details are in your packet. You'll take the SUV with tinted windows." Anne Marie swiveled around and pinned her predatory gaze on someone else, but Harris tuned out the orders she was barking. He rifled through the folder until he found Candice's itinerary. She was landing at the Lexington airport early two Sundays from now. Smart. It was a smallish airport favored by business commuters, so there wouldn't be a lot of traffic on a Sunday morning.

He didn't relish leaving at the asscrack of dawn to go get her, so maybe he'd spend the night with Jackson and Jordan next week so he could leave for the airport from their place.

Sleeping in the same apartment as Jackson would be a special torture. Harris had only done it half a dozen times, and the experience always left him both wishing he hadn't stayed and wishing he could stay longer. It was hard for his wolf when their scents mingled, though having Jordan's scent in the mix tempered things a little. He wasn't sure he'd be able to hold back without it. It would take the situation from uncomfortable to unbearable.

He tuned back in as Anne Marie was wrapping up. Everyone had special projects to work on to ready the campers and the camp itself for Candice's arrival. The wolflings had all been raised to respect other Weres' privacy and keep the secret, but this was a big secret to keep. Their gooey little brains weren't fully formed yet, but impulsive behavior would get everyone in a lot of trouble.

"Harris, we're hiring Fang and Fury to do a security audit and beef up the protection around the camp. I'm putting you on point with that since you're friends with them. Find out their installation plans and let me know. We'll put them up for as long as it takes, of course. They can stay with Drew."

Harris's heart leaped. Fang and Fury was Jackson and Jordan's private security firm, which meant Jackson was coming to Camp H.O.W.L., maybe for several days. They must have been hired recently since Jackson hadn't mentioned it last time they talked.

"Will do."

"The system is due some upgrades anyway, so don't worry too much about a budget. We'll make it work somehow, especially since if we handle this right, we could get more high-profile wolflings. They pay a premium for the extra security, and I like being one of the few camps in the country who can accommodate them."

Camp H.O.W.L. was one of the premiere camps in the US, if not the world. They had kids come from all over, including overseas, to take advantage of the Olympic-quality athletic facilities, the luxury cabins, and the chef Anne Marie had poached from a Michelin-rated restaurant. The quality of the food was wasted on the palate of the average nineteen-year-old, as evidenced by the food fights that broke out and the number of times kids tried to order a pizza and have it delivered to the secret werewolf camp in the middle of a national forest. Harris despaired of the future sometimes. Then again, the kids were going through the most stressful thing in their young lives—the Turn. A few weeks ago, their bodies were human. Weres had no physiological difference from humans until they entered the Turn the first full moon after their nineteenth birthday. These kids were experiencing super senses and getting to know a whole different body on top of the usual teenage hormones. It was a miracle anyone made it out alive.

Security around the camp was already serious, so Harris had a hard time imagining how it could be tightened. Then again, that was literally what Jackson and Jordan did with their security business, Fang and Fury. If there were weaknesses in Camp H.O.W.L.'s security, they would find them.

"I'm heading over to Lexington to see them tomorrow," Harris said. "I'll confirm everything with them and make sure they're all set with their credentials."

They were both frequent visitors to the camp, but the security system required updated tokens to gain entrance. For staffers in Camp H.O.W.L. cars, the beacons installed in the vehicles were enough to trigger the facial recognition camera, which allowed them in. Visitors had temporary tokens and were buzzed in by whomever was manning the control center. It was a pain sometimes, but it kept the wolflings safe and the werewolf secret under wraps. They were free to run around the camp shifted with no fear of exposure, which was practically unheard of anywhere else.

"I was going to mail them a long-term token, but if you're going over, you can take it. They'll be coming and going a lot, and I don't want to keep issuing temporary tokens, especially since they might need to access the control center in a crisis. Tell Jackson he should work on getting them added to the visual recognition software." She paused and frowned. "If he thinks it's a good idea, of course."

Harris had never seen Anne Marie defer to *anyone* for any reason and was surprised she'd put so much trust in Jackson and Jordan.

She must have picked up on his curiosity. "Part of Candice's requests was to have Fang and Fury provide security assistance while she was here. They've made a big name for themselves in the supernatural world. I was planning to hire them for our upgrade anyway, so this just moved my timeline forward. I've been around Jackson enough to know he's a trustworthy guy, and Jordan gets on my last ever-loving nerve, but his instincts are good. They're a good fit for us."

She had no idea how true that was. Harris had been friends with Jackson, Jordan, and Drew since college— and lusting after Jackson for nearly that long. Being with them was easy. There was no other way to explain it. Jackson, Jordan, and Drew felt like home to him, which was ironic because St. Louis *wasn't* his home. He'd grown up in the San Francisco Pack. He was still on the books as a Pack member there, though he hadn't been back in years.

Why go back when he had everything he needed here? Drew liked to joke that Harris was a common-law member of the Garrison Pack in St. Louis, since he went to a good number of the Pack ceremonies and celebrations. He liked the Pack well enough, but Jackson was the real reason he kept going. And Drew and Jordan. But mostly Jackson.

And now he was going to spend the day with him *and* at least part of a week with him next week. Starlet or not, things were looking up.

Chapter Two

JACKSON hauled his duffel bag up on his shoulder and pushed through the crowd at the gate. He'd been up for forty-eight hours, and he didn't have any patience for the people chattering around him.

He hadn't checked any baggage for his two-day trip to New York for his interview with the Werewolf Tribunal. His usual uniform of a polo shirt and cargo pants had been as dressy as he needed to be, especially since most of his interview took place on a sparring mat in the Tribunal Enforcer gym.

Jackson nearly wept with relief when he saw Jordan's car waiting at the curb. Jordan could be a gigantic flake sometimes, but he almost always came through when it was important.

"You look like warmed-over shit," Jordan said when Jackson opened the door and slid into the front seat.

"Then I look better than I feel," Jackson muttered. He tossed his duffel over his shoulder into the back and slumped against the seat.

"That bad?"

"Worse," Jackson said. He closed his eyes, which felt dry and scratchy from his lack of sleep and the recycled air on the plane. "The interview lasted a day and a half."

Jordan whistled through his teeth. "That's a lot of meetings."

"No," Jackson said, cracking one eye open to look at him. "That's *one* meeting that went for thirty-six hours. They were looking at how I handled stress."

"Damn. What did they do?"

"After the face-to-face interview, I sparred with a few Enforcers, and then they had me research some cold cases. After that I was put in a hood and dumped on some Pack land outside the city. There was an obstacle course, and once I completed it, more sparring and some shifting drills. Then I had to find my own way back to the Tribunal headquarters."

"That's one toughass interview."

It was, but there was a good reason for it. Tribunal Enforcers were the best of the best. There were twenty district Enforcers applying for the open spot, and all of them had impressive track records in their own region. Jackson had tough competition for the job.

"You made it back, though."

"I did. And as soon as I got back they took me to the airport and told me they'd be in touch in a few weeks."

"That's kind of fucked."

"The test or the wait time?"

"Both," Jordan said, and Jackson snorted out a laugh. "It's the big leagues."

"Sucks you have to wait, but since you're going to be here for at least the next few weeks, I guess I should tell you I signed with a new client while you were gone."

Jackson sighed and rubbed a hand over his face, sitting up. "Can this wait until tomorrow?"

"Tomorrow Harris is coming, and I know better than to expect you'll get anything done with him around."

Jackson's stomach lurched. He'd forgotten Harris was coming. They'd made the plans weeks ago, well before the Tribunal Enforcer job had opened up. Jackson hadn't told him he had applied. He usually told Harris everything, but for some reason he'd held this close to his chest. He'd told Drew, but he'd asked his stepbrother not to mention it to anyone else. Jackson needed to be the one to tell Harris.

"What's the job?"

"High-profile camper. Anne Marie sent over the file. We're going to need to do a full overhaul and come up with some new security protocols."

That must mean *high* profile, then. They made the two-and-a-half-hour drive a few times a year to clear the camp when a tycoon's kid or some foreign royal came to Camp H.O.W.L., but they usually had more lead time than this.

"Last minute?"

"They didn't want the news to leak, so her parents didn't enroll her until Thursday."

Fuck. An upgrade at Camp H.O.W.L. would usually take a month or more to plan. Luckily things were pretty solid there, but there were additional layers Fang and Fury would have to put in place and not a lot of time to do it.

"Who's the camper?"

Jordan's face lit up, so Jackson knew this was going to be bad.

"Kandie Bates."

The name didn't ring a bell. Jackson kept track of all the prominent Were families because Pack politics was an important component of his job. He knew a lot of the Weres in both government and entertainment, but only because Fang and Fury had worked for most of them.

"She's an actress. Her parents are going to bring us on to consult on her personal security and exposure risks after she finishes at Camp H.O.W.L."

"They'll be bringing *you* on. I'm going to be moving to New York, and Tribunal Enforcers aren't allowed to freelance."

"Or have Pack bonds or relationships or anything that would make them like the rest of us mere mortals, I know," Jordan said. He'd turned away, but Jackson could hear the eye roll in his voice.

Jordan didn't want him to go out for the Tribunal job because it meant he'd have to leave the Garrison Pack, and it pissed Jackson off that Jordan couldn't see why it was so important. "There's a good reason for all that."

"You don't have to cut ties to be a regional Enforcer. I don't see how it's any different."

Jackson ignored him and settled back into his seat. They'd had this argument half a dozen times since Jackson applied for the job. Jordan kept talking, but Jackson sank into his exhaustion and fell asleep.

"WHY are you cleaning?"

Jackson pulled his head out of the microwave and scowled at Jordan, who'd hopped up onto the counter and was eating a muffin.

He'd slept most of Saturday, recovering from his Tribunal Enforcer interview, and woken bright and early this morning in a panic because the apartment was a mess and Harris was coming.

"Harris will be here soon, remember?"

Jordan arched a brow at him and took another messy bite. Jackson's fingers twitched to knock the muffin out of his hands. There were crumbs all over the floor he'd just swept.

"Whassa big deal?" he asked around his muffin. "It's just Harry."

Jackson finished wiping the dried-up gunk in the microwave—courtesy of Jordan reheating chili last week without a lid—and threw the sponge in the sink. "He doesn't like it when you call him that. Don't be a dick the second he walks in the door, okay? Give it at least ten minutes before you make him want to commit homicide."

Jordan shoved the remainder of the muffin in his mouth and dusted his shirt and hands off onto the floor as he hopped down. "Be a shame if you had to arrest him," he said sweetly.

Jackson smacked Jordan's hand as he reached for a bag of chips. "I will fucking *help him* if you don't stop making messes!"

They'd grown up almost as close as brothers, so living with Jordan hadn't been much of a transition when they moved into a place together in Lexington. But there was a difference between living with Jordan and *living with* Jordan, and it was sometimes hard to manage both. He was a disgusting slob. Jackson wasn't a neat freak, but he'd classify his housekeeping style as more "living out of clean laundry baskets instead of putting the clothes away" as opposed to Jordan's "host a house party for cockroaches" approach.

They'd made it three years without ruining their friendship, but Jackson didn't know how much longer that would last. Another reason to hope his application to transfer to the Enforcer headquarters at the East Coast Tribunal was accepted.

Jordan had been itching to move back to St. Louis, and if Jackson moved to New York, nothing would be keeping him here. Right now, Jackson was a Tribunal Enforcer in Lexington, which was great. He enjoyed the work he did, and it allowed him to keep his full-time job with the police department. But a spot at the Tribunal headquarters for a regional Enforcer had opened up, and he wanted it. As part of the East Coast Tribunal's Enforcer squad, he'd be working cases that were more important and higher profile. It was a way for him to scout around and get to know different Packs too. He'd need to make a name for himself if he wanted to be a Pack Second someday.

The screech of the oven timer drew him out of his funk, and Jackson grabbed the pair of wolf-shaped pot holders Harris had given him as a housewarming present to take the cinnamon rolls he'd been baking out of the oven.

"We're literally going to lunch as soon as he gets here," Jordan said. He reached out to snag one, and Jackson grabbed his arm and twisted him into a rear wristlock, making Jordan yelp in pain. "Fine, fine. I won't touch his precious cinnamon rolls."

Jackson let him go, and Jordan rubbed at his wrist even though his Were healing would have kicked in the moment Jackson released him. Such a drama queen.

"You are aware you've been possessed by June Cleaver, right? I mean, you were up at like seven this morning doing laundry. And I could eat off every surface in this apartment, it's so clean—"

Jackson looked up from icing the cinnamon rolls and bared his teeth. "Try it."

"—and now you're freaking *baking*. What is up with you, dude? You know Harris doesn't care if there are socks on the lampshades."

Jackson sighed. "There should never be socks on lampshades, Jordan. And I was up early because I realized we don't have clean sheets. What if he decides to stay over?"

Jordan snorted. "He's not going to stay over. You have to work tomorrow. Why is he coming anyway? We'll be down at Camp H.O.W.L. on Monday. You two can braid each other's hair and share gossip about cute boys then."

Jackson took a breath and reminded himself that he enjoyed working for Fang and Fury, even if his boss was a total asshole. Reporting to Jordan was an exercise in patience. Luckily, the work was interesting and part-time. Most of his coworkers at the station freelanced, so it wasn't a big deal when Jackson needed to switch shifts to accommodate a Fang and Fury client. He did it for plenty of other officers for their off-duty gigs.

Jordan tossed a pot holder at him when Jackson didn't respond. "I'm just saying, I hate it when you flirt in the living room. The stink lingers for days."

The temptation to put Jordan in a hold again was strong. Maybe even handcuff him to something in Jordan's room so he would leave Jackson alone. He'd done it before. Jordan had snapped them, and Jackson had to pay for the replacement cuffs out of his own pocket. He couldn't explain that his roommate had used werewolf strength to break the steel, so he'd had to tell his commanding officer he lost them.

"He wanted to go to that Korean place he likes so much," Jackson said. "And you make it sound like it's a big deal. It's just a two-hour drive. We don't live on the moon."

Jordan stroked his chin. "What *would* happen if we lived on the moon, do you think? I mean, would it be like the pull of a full moon all the time? Do you think there have been any werewolf astronauts?"

Jackson was used to Jordan's non sequiturs and didn't bother answering. He'd be musing about a new topic any second now.

He busied himself putting the cinnamon rolls on a plate. Jordan was right—he *was* acting weird. He was amped up and unable to settle. Little things like the chili in the microwave were unusually infuriating. It was almost like nesting.

It had to be stress about the promotion. He'd flown out for the interview a week ago, and they told him they'd get back to him in a month. There was no point worrying about it—either he had the job or he didn't. Nothing else he could do about it right now. Except clean his apartment, apparently.

Down the hall, the elevator swished open, and he focused his hearing further, picking Harris's heartbeat out as he walked down the hall. Some of his nervous energy settled knowing Harris was here.

Jackson was finishing up with the rolls as Harris unlocked the front door with his key. Jackson had never really thought about why he trusted Harris with one before now. Drew had one, since he was Jackson's stepbrother, but even Jackson's former boyfriend Raoul hadn't been given that kind of free access to their place.

But when the landlord had asked how many keys they'd needed, he'd answered four without thinking. Huh.

Harris's scent arrived in the kitchen a second before he walked in, and it hit Jackson like a punch to the gut. Harris smelled tired but good. Like a pine forest in a storm—heady, with the faintest hint of ozone and smoke. He'd never noticed before.

Harris's eyes widened at the sight of the plate. "You baked? What's the occasion?"

You visiting, he almost said, but he swallowed the words. The last thing he needed was Harris teasing him for being such a weirdo.

"Just felt like it. I always like to bake when I clean. It makes the place smell better."

That was true. Harsh chemical air fresheners wreaked havoc on sensitive Were noses, and his stepmother had always baked a pie or cookies when the funk of four teenage boys under one roof got too heavy.

But he'd had an odd drive to make the place nice for Harris. It was strange.

Harris reached out and took a cinnamon roll, and Jordan made a sharp noise.

"So, he can eat them but I can't?"

Harris paused with the cinnamon roll halfway to his mouth, brow quirked in question. His lips looked a little chapped but still gorgeous, and the playful expression on his face made Jackson's heart do a funny little skip.

"You can have one, asswipe. I just didn't want you eating one before I even had them on the plate," he said, shoving the plate toward Jordan.

He didn't care for the challenging look Jordan gave him, so he ignored it.

Harris made an appreciative humming noise, and Jackson turned back in time to see his eyes fluttering closed as he chewed. Jackson turned away and busied himself shoving the oven mitts into a drawer. Not the one they belonged in, but Harris wouldn't know that. Hell, Jordan didn't know that. Jackson made a mental note to grab them and put them in their proper place later.

"You didn't tell me Fang and Fury picked up a contract at Camp H.O.W.L.," Harris said after he'd swallowed.

"I didn't know until Jordan picked me up yesterday."

Fuck. He hadn't meant to say it like that. Any hope that Harris hadn't heard him was dashed when he raised an eyebrow. "Something wrong with your car?"

"He didn't want to pay airport parking, and I, being the fine specimen of a roommate that I am, offered to drive him."

"I was in New York," Jackson said before Harris could ask for more details. It was better to do this fast. "I had an interview. A Tribunal Enforcer job opened up, and they liked my application."

Harris stared at him for a moment, his expression stricken, before his face smoothed into the mask Jackson saw him use in therapy. Shit. He was mad.

"The Tribunal Enforcers work out of the East Coast headquarters, right?"

Jackson nodded. His heart was in his throat, and he couldn't seem to force words past it. If Harris disapproved—well, he wouldn't take his name out of the running, but he wouldn't feel good about taking the job either. Harris's opinion meant a lot.

"Well, I'm sure you'll get it," Harris said, his mask still in place. "They'll be lucky to have you."

They fell into silence until Jordan broke it by clapping his hands together.

"You have everything you need to play some basketball after lunch, Harry?" Jordan smiled when

Jackson glared at him. Jackson's department was having a pickup tournament, and Jackson had decided to skip it because Harris was visiting. Jordan wanted to go, though, hence his meddling.

Harris glanced down at his feet. "I'm wearing sneakers, which I'm more than willing to put up your ass if you call me Harry again."

Jackson snickered. He was the only one allowed to call Harris by any sort of nickname. Probably because he did it affectionately. Jordan did it to be a dick.

"Should be fine. I'll need to borrow some sweats, though."

Jordan grinned in triumph. "Jackson, you heard the man. Go grab him some clothes."

Jackson's stomach leaped at the thought of Harris in his clothes. "You go grab him some clothes."

Jordan's shit-eating smile grew. "You're the only one who has anything clean. I haven't done laundry in like, two weeks."

Bastard. He'd planned this. Jordan was an annoying little shit sometimes. Fuck. Make that most of the time. Apparently, Jackson hadn't been as good at hiding his growing crush as he'd thought.

"It's just an intradepartmental pickup game," he said. "It's nothing important. We can skip it."

Harris's eyes lit up, and Jackson was done for. "I'll get to meet the guys you work with? Hell yeah, I'm in. You've been talking about them for three years. I want to put names to faces."

Jackson sighed and retreated to his bedroom, praying Jordan behaved himself. Who was he kidding? Jordan never behaved. But hopefully he'd keep his new revelations to himself.

The gym they played in was always sweltering, so he grabbed an old department T-shirt and a pair of loose mesh shorts for Harris. It didn't escape his notice he'd chosen a shirt with his name on the back. Part of him wanted to mark Harris as his. Even though he wasn't. Jesus. He was usually better at compartmentalizing.

He tossed the bundle to Harris, who raised his hands to catch it. He was wearing a pair of tight jeans and a V-neck T-shirt that was mouthwateringly fitted. Jackson had always been one to appreciate a fine male body, and Harris definitely had one. So did Jordan and nearly every Were he knew. But he'd always been able downplay his attraction to Harris before. They'd been spending more time together lately, and it was getting increasingly difficult not to drool over him.

His wolf was going crazy at the thought of Harris wearing his things. Sweat trickled down his back, and his body felt tender and hot, like the shift was prickling at his skin. It had never been like this with Raoul or his other boyfriends. He had no idea what was going on or why it was directed at one of his best friends. A mix of anxiety and homesickness, perhaps, and all of it focused on Harris because he was always such a comforting, solid presence.

Jackson snorted. That was all bullshit. He had a good old-fashioned crush, and he couldn't explain it away as his worry over the new job.

No, this was carnal lust mixed with affection. Dammit.

It was ridiculous. They'd been friends for over a decade. Harris was good-looking, and Jackson had been appreciative of that since they met. But it was just that—attraction. He wouldn't throw away their friendship for a fuck. Harris was worth more than that.

He deserved someone who could give him more than a casual relationship—someone who wasn't married to his career and had room in his life for Harris. Jackson's dedication to rising through the Enforcer ranks had been the reason he and Raoul broke up two months ago. And also the reason he hadn't cared, aside from the inconvenience of losing his regular bed partner.

God, he was such a dick.

Harris and Jordan were staring at him, and Jackson realized they were waiting on him to see what they were doing next. Time to stop thinking and get on with the day.

"Let's go get lunch," he told them.

WATCHING Harris use chopsticks was bad enough, but seeing him hip check a dude who had forty pounds on him while wearing a sweat-soaked T-shirt— *Jackson's* T-shirt—was rock bottom. Jackson was grateful he was on the bench right now because his thin shorts did nothing to disguise how interested he was.

No one had blinked at Jackson bringing Harris along to play. They were used to Jordan trailing along behind him. He'd hoped his chief would say no to a civilian joining, but he'd just slapped Harris on the back and asked him how strong his three-pointer was.

The answer was, strong. Jackson knew Harris was good since they played pickup games with the Pack in St. Louis, but the way Harris moved with such grace— it was almost art. He was constantly in motion and deadly accurate with his shots.

Harris came away from a rebound scuffle with possession of the ball and pivoted, a look of complete concentration on his face while he lined up his shot and let it go. He bit at his bottom lip as he watched it arc, and Jackson would have given anything to do the same right now.

"You doing okay there, Berrings?"

Jackson flinched. He hadn't heard his CO sit down next to him. This obsession with Harris was fucking with his senses.

"Yeah, just woolgathering."

"You're in next. That friend you brought is something. I don't suppose he'd want to join the team?"

God no. Jackson couldn't handle seeing this weekly. "He's just visiting. Besides, he's a therapist, not a cop."

Harris blocked a shot and grabbed the ball, darting around the other team like it was an open court. No one could stop him. "Coulda fooled me," Jackson's CO said, gaping at the sight on the court. "Guy's tough. He's had law enforcement training somewhere. You can tell by the way he carries himself."

It was a common mistake. Weres stood tall and were always on alert—they were often taken for military or law enforcement out in public. It was a byproduct of their senses. Even though they worked hard not to react to every little thing out in public, it was impossible to turn it off.

"He's done a little personal security work," Jackson said when it was clear his CO was expecting an answer. It wasn't a lie. All Camp H.O.W.L. staffers patrolled and provided general security on the property.

Jackson flinched when a whistle blew a few feet away. Jordan smirked at him from the court.

"Berrings, you're in for Michaelson. Good luck, son."

Fuck. Of all the players to sub in for, it had to be the one guarding Harris? He ignored Jordan's quiet snickers and jogged onto the court.

"Ooh, this should be fun," Harris teased when he took his place next to him. They'd paused for a water break, and Jackson had to bite back an admonishment that Harris needed to drink more to keep himself hydrated. He was a grown man. If he wanted to get a drink, he'd get a drink.

"Don't think I'm going to take it easy on you because we're friends, Harry," Jackson said, satisfaction bubbling up inside him when Harris's ears flushed at the nickname. "You're going down."

Harris shot him a wicked grin. "It *is* a particular talent of mine," he said as the whistle blew and play resumed.

Jackson stood there stunned as Harris blew past him, getting into position for Jordan to pass to him. Jackson followed a beat later, moving faster than he should in a room full of humans. The burn in his muscles from honest-to-God exertion felt amazing. And the thrill of chasing his mate—

Jackson stopped dead at the thought. A pass from Carlson smacked against the side of his face and he went down hard, slamming his shoulder into the court when he fell.

Play kept going, but Harris was at his side in an instant. "Fuck, Jackson," he said, breathless. "What is up with you, man? Are you all right? Do you need to see Drew?"

Jackson laughed humorlessly. He'd like to see Drew, but not because he needed a checkup. His brother was newly mated, and Jackson had a lot of questions for him—and for his partner Nick, who was a Were.

He'd thought of Harris as his *mate*. That was a big Freudian slip. He'd never given much thought to finding a mate because his career was so important. Why the hell was his brain taking him there now? And with Harris? This was fucked on so many levels.

He took the hand Harris offered him, letting him pull him up off the court. His CO beckoned them over, and for the sake of appearances, Jackson leaned into Harris, playing along as Harris helped him shuffle off the court. A human would probably have a concussion. He'd have to call Drew and ask.

"Shit, Berrings. When I said get your head in the game, I didn't mean literally," his CO barked. "Go get that checked out."

He looked at Harris, who was still holding Jackson up. Jackson gave in and leaned into the touch, heat flaring through him at the close contact.

"Harris, right? Can you take him? If Jordan leaves it will mess up the rotation."

"Sure, no problem," Harris said without hesitation. His concern wasn't faked. It oozed off him, mixed with confusion.

"Have his head checked out," the man said gruffly before turning to shout at players on the court.

"I'll get a ride home. You guys can take off," Jordan said quietly. He didn't look at them, and anyone near him would think he was mumbling to himself.

Perfect. Now Jackson had to head back to the apartment alone with Harris. His dick twitched at the thought. Maybe he *did* need to have his head examined.

HARRIS stuck around until Jordan got back, which was hours after the game had ended, the fucker. Jackson managed not to embarrass himself, but only just. They played video games and ate all the cinnamon rolls, and Harris had insisted Jackson call Drew.

His stepbrother agreed a human would have a concussion and wrote him a doctor's note to that effect.

Department policy meant he was on leave until a doctor cleared him, but since he'd already put in for vacation so he and Jordan could work at Camp H.O.W.L. for a few days, it didn't really matter.

JACKSON tossed and turned, unable to get comfortable no matter what position he tried. He'd never had problems sleeping before, even when he was in the middle of horrific cases. Every time he closed his eyes he thought about Harris, which wasn't conducive to mellowing out and falling asleep.

It had to be stress.

He was so damn tired of waiting for the call from the Tribunal. He knew they were working their way across the country, interviewing potential regional Enforcers, and that took time. But it didn't help settle his nerves knowing they might be talking to someone who was a better fit for the position right now.

Well, not right this minute. He rolled over and looked at his phone on the nightstand, groaning. It was three in the morning. He and Jordan were leaving for Camp H.O.W.L. in three hours to meet with the staff to talk about some of the changes they'd be making to the security system.

They'd be there most of the week, tweaking procedures and adding new cameras and sensors so everything was secure for the new high-profile camper. It was larger scale than most of the security overhauls Fang and Fury had done, but it wasn't all that difficult. Or rather, the work wasn't difficult. Having Harris so close after the alarming realization that he saw him as mate material was a different story.

Jackson was a master at compartmentalization. It was what made him a good cop, and it made him an excellent Enforcer. It would also make him a great Second for a Pack. When he was at work, he was at work. Period.

But all afternoon he'd zoned out, admiring the curve of Harris's jaw or getting lost in his scent, and that was going to be a real problem if they were working together.

Jackson gave up on sleep after twenty more frustrating minutes of staring at the ceiling. He padded into the kitchen and took out the box of tea Harris kept stashed in the cupboard. It was a special blend he'd been drinking for as long as they'd known each other, and Jackson had given him plenty of shit over the years for preferring the loose tea. He pulled the lid off and sniffed the fragrant leaves. Tension flowed out of him as he took another deep inhale.

He was debating making himself a cup when the floorboards squeaked. Jackson whirled around, shoving the tea behind him on the counter, but he could tell from Jordan's shit-eating grin he'd been caught.

"Something keeping you up?"

Jackson considered lying, but it was the middle of the night, and he'd had his nose in another man's tea tin. He flushed at the thought. It sounded like a euphemism for what he'd been fantasizing about doing to Harris.

"Just worried about the job I applied for."

Jordan hummed and bobbed his head. He opened the cabinet and pulled out a bottle of Jameson. "I know ice cream is the traditional let's-talk-about-boys offering, but you haven't been to the store lately."

Jordan poured generous helpings of whiskey into two tumblers. He shelved the bottle before offering Jackson one, which must mean he really was concerned. He only cleaned up after himself when Jackson was upset.

"Wanna tell me what's up? I mean, I know how invested you are in this Tribunal job, but come on, Jackson. You've been an airhead all day, and your heart was going crazy when I came home tonight."

Jackson took a sip and held it against the top of his palate, enjoying the burn. It wouldn't get him drunk, but he still liked the taste. He wanted to shift and run from this conversation on four legs, but that would just make things worse.

"I'm working through some things."

Jordan smirked. "*Some things* like how you want to jump Harris?"

Jackson slumped against the counter.

"Yeah, it's obvious. Some of the guys asked if he was your boyfriend after you two left together. Harris definitely didn't notice. But he's been gone on you as long as I've known him, so maybe that's why he's so oblivious."

Jackson knew Harris was attracted to him. That kind of thing was impossible to hide around Weres. But Harris had never done anything to make Jackson believe it was more than just that—attraction. Jackson knew he smelled the same way around Harris and untold numbers of other people. That didn't mean he wanted to pursue it, and Were etiquette demanded ignoring it unless the other person brought it up.

"Even if he is, the timing's shit. With any luck, I'll be moving to New York in a month." He ran a hand through his hair, tugging on the strands in frustration. He needed a haircut, but Harris liked it longer, and he'd been putting it off.

God. This wasn't a recent thing.

"He's one of my best friends. I can't ruin that after a decade because my wolf wants to claim him."

Jordan's eyebrows rose. "Your wolf wants to claim him?"

Shit. He hadn't meant to say that.

"Listen, Jackson," Jordan said, his tone softer. "You know the wolf is *you*. Your instincts might be baser when you're thinking with that part of your nature, but it's still very much you. Take it from me. I lost your brother because I was fighting my instincts. But I was really fighting myself. Our wolves aren't a separate entity. If your instincts are pulling you toward him, then it's because your heart and your brain think he's something special."

"And my dick," Jackson murmured with a scowl.

"That too," Jordan said, his voice thick with laughter. "I mean, if that's the only part of you that's driving this—"

"It's not."

"I didn't think so. If that were the case you wouldn't be smelling his tea in the middle of the night."

"I've been denying it, but I'm nesting." The words hung heavy, weighing against his chest like an anvil.

Jordan made a sympathetic sound. "You know what that means."

"I see him as a potential mate. But I don't want a mate. I'm not ready for one. I have so much more I need to accomplish before I'm ready to settle down."

"So here we are."

"Here we are," Jackson agreed. He gulped down the rest of his whiskey. "Don't tell him about the tea."

Chapter Three

"**HE** hasn't talked to you about what's bothering him?"

Drew took the top sheet from the pile of linens in Harris's arms and snapped it over the bed. Even the bottom sheets in Drew's linen closet were expertly folded. The man was clearly a laundry ninja. Harris would have to ask him for tips.

"No, but he's still waiting to hear on that job. That's got to be nerve-racking."

Harris put down his bundle of blankets and towels on a nearby chair and helped Drew tuck the corners of the sheet in. He hadn't helped prepare Jordan's room, aside from holding the stuff, but he liked the idea of his scent on Jackson's sheets. Making up his bed was domestic and made Harris's inner wolf purr with contentment.

"Totally. But you didn't see him, Drew. He was so distracted. He let that basketball hit him. I don't think he saw it coming at all. It was bizarre."

Drew snickered. "I *wish* I'd seen it. It was funny enough hearing about the aftermath, though. It's probably a good thing he's going to be here instead of patrolling if he's that out of it. Remind me to write him a note releasing him for duty when they leave."

"If he's doing better," Harris said as he smoothed wrinkles out of the quilt. "I don't want him out there in the line of duty if he's still so distracted."

"He'll hear from the Tribunal soon. But yeah, I agree. We'll see how it goes."

Harris resisted the urge to rub his face over the pillow as he tucked it into a case, but he rubbed his wrist across the breadth of it. There was no way Jackson wouldn't notice his scent on it, but it wasn't so heavy it couldn't have been from making the bed. Stealth scent marking was a skill he'd been perfecting since he'd figured out Jackson was his mate two years ago.

Harris took the pile of towels on the chair into the guest suite bathroom and hung them on the rack. Jackson always stayed in this room when he visited, and Drew always let Harris help him make the bed and get things in order. He knew Harris had a major crush on his stepbrother, but Harris had never told him the extent of it. Only Adrian and Tate knew the whole story, and Harris intended to keep it that way. He didn't want to see sympathy—or worse, pity—on Drew's face every time he looked at him, or risk making things weird between them. It wouldn't be fair to make Drew feel like he had to be disloyal to his own brother by keeping secrets.

Harris spent a few minutes tidying up the bathroom, putting the toiletries Jackson kept at the house for his visits out on the counter and wiping at a smudge on the mirror. He didn't take this many pains in his own bathroom, but this was one of the rare opportunities he had to take care of his mate, so he indulged himself.

"You want tea before the meeting?" Drew called from the bedroom.

"Yeah, and maybe a bagel or something. I'm starving."

The usual Monday morning staff breakfast had been canceled to make time for Fang and Fury's presentation about the new security procedures. No one was happy about missing out on pancakes, but the kitchen had promised a nice continental breakfast buffet to make up for it. Food would be arriving soon.

Harris had already been for a run before he wandered over to the infirmary to help Drew set up for the meeting and make up rooms for Jackson and Jordan. He'd woken up at five after a night of unsettling dreams.

He'd regret that tonight when he fell asleep over his reports, but he'd been too anxious to try to fight the insomnia. The prospect of having Jackson on campus all week should've been exciting, but the butterflies in his stomach were more worried than happy.

Drew had a cup of tea steeping on the counter by the time Harris made it down to the kitchen. He was tucking his phone back in his pocket.

"Jackson says they're about twenty minutes out. Breakfast was delivered, so I'm going to get that set up."

It stung that Jackson hadn't called him, but he understood. Drew was his brother, and that trumped best friend. Though usually he sent a group text.

Harris followed Drew to the kitchen, where big platters of danishes, fruit, and other treats were sitting. He picked up the large urn of coffee as Drew reached for it, earning himself a glare.

"Before you say anything, I didn't take this because you're a fragile human."

Drew reached for a platter of bagels, cream cheese, and lox. Harris waited until he was already walking before adding, "I took it because you're clumsy as fuck, and I need this coffee to keep me going."

Drew tossed half a bagel over his shoulder at him, and it plopped to the ground a few feet shy of its target.

"I'm not clumsy. The floor is warped here. You could trip too, asshole."

Harris very much doubted that, unless Jackson was nearby.

BY the time everyone had finished breakfast and Jackson and Jordan had given their overview of the security changes, Harris was ready to jump out of his skin. Jackson looked cool and confident as he laid out the new procedures, but his heart was going wild and his scent was laced with the sour tang of anxiety and panic.

Anyone who didn't know him intimately would write it off as stage fright from speaking to a large group, but Jackson loved things like this. He normally radiated authority and calm—it was what was going to make him a kick-ass Second someday. Harris had no idea what was going on with him.

"He's twitchy," Drew murmured when they broke for more coffee. Jackson was handing out individual schedules for the new security rounds they'd start when Candice arrived. Everyone would patrol in pairs, and the routes and times would change every day. It was a big departure from how they usually did things.

"I told you," Harris answered. He pulled Drew into the hallway, not letting go until they reached the relative privacy of the kitchen. The rumble of a dozen different conversations in the other room would mask theirs. "He was like this all day yesterday too. *Before* getting hit in the head. Do you still think this is just stress?"

Drew's brow furrowed. "I don't know. Maybe? I'll talk to him."

Relief trickled through Harris. Something was wrong with his mate, and he wouldn't rest until he found out what it was and fixed it. Having Drew on board made that a lot easier.

"YOU can't just trade security detail times."

Harris rolled his eyes at Jackson's back as he followed him down the trail Jordan had carved out earlier in the week. He and Jackson had been at Camp H.O.W.L. for three days, working from sunup to sundown laying these routes for the new patrols. The trails relied more on scent than anything—the actual path was only a few inches wide. Just enough to cut through the brush to help guide them in the beginning. Eventually, the woods would retake the trail, but by then their scent would saturate the trees and ground. The idea was to make these patrol routes invisible to humans, since odds were good it would be a human who tried to break in.

"I haven't seen you all week. You're not even taking meals in the mess. I had to resort to some middle-school bullshit to get you alone." Harris didn't even try to disguise the anger in his tone.

"The security details are set up to pair you with someone who is strong in your weak areas. Jordan and I put a lot of work into matching people up, and you've got to start patrolling with your partner to get a routine going."

Harris knew that. But he was paired with Luke, the camp's agility instructor, and the two of them already had a good relationship. Harris was a better tracker and had better control over his wolf, but Luke was flexible as fuck and fast. Incredibly fast. There was no question about how they'd patrol together. Luke would take the outer path and sprint, and Harris would shift and follow the interweaving inside paths as a wolf. They'd have the benefit of Harris's keen hearing and sense of smell paired with Luke's ability to cover more ground and his eyesight, which could pick out more detail than a wolf could in shifted form.

"I'll put in some extra time with him tomorrow," Harris said. "Besides, Jordan is wiped. He literally fell asleep at dinner tonight. He needed a break." *So do you*, Harris thought, but he knew better than to start a fight over Jackson's work ethic. He gave 110 percent of himself to every job. It was a huge part of who Jackson was, and Harris couldn't imagine him any other way.

Jackson stopped and turned around. It was the closest they'd been all week, and up close the bags under his eyes and the waxy pallor of his skin became obvious. Jackson was running on fumes.

"Hey," Harris said, reaching out and squeezing Jackson's shoulder. "I'm sure Anne Marie appreciates how much work you're putting in, but you've got to take care of yourself. You should head back to Drew's and get some sleep. I'll cover the patrol."

He'd spent days trying to get Jackson alone, and now he was pushing him away. But Harris's instincts were telling him he needed to take care of his mate, and that trumped his desire to get answers about Jackson's weird behavior.

"Protocol is no one patrols alone," Jackson mumbled. His eyes were glassy and unfocused, and he looked like he was about to fall asleep right where he stood.

"The new security rules aren't actually in effect until Monday. Go to bed, Jackson."

Jackson swayed and then blinked hard, shaking his head. "I don't want to leave you out here alone."

What was there to be afraid of? Harris was the biggest predator out there. Or at least he would be as soon as he got Jackson to bed. "I'll be fine."

Jackson bit his lip, and Harris's libido went from zero to sixty. He swallowed hard and forced his gaze up to Jackson's red-rimmed, exhausted eyes. Nothing sexy there.

"I miss you," Jackson blurted out, the words slurred.

Was it possible to get drunk from exhaustion?

"I miss you too, man. You've been really busy this week. C'mon. Let's get you to Drew's before you pass out."

Jackson leaned into him, and Harris wrapped an arm around his waist. He started walking back the way they'd come, relieved when Jackson stumbled along with him.

"I'm not, you know," Jackson muttered.

Harris huffed out a laugh. "Not what? C'mon, you're dead on your feet."

"Busy," Jackson said. "I'm not that busy. It hurts to be around you. I want to be with you all the time, but I'm so mad at you."

Harris tripped over a tree root and had to tighten his hold on Jackson to keep himself from going sprawling. He'd known Jackson was avoiding him, but he hadn't realized Jackson was actually *mad* at him. Harris scoured his mind for anything he might have done to upset Jackson this much. His heart sat heavy in his chest at the thought of hurting his mate.

He wondered if Jackson would even remember telling him that tomorrow. Harris wanted to press for more details, but he didn't want to take advantage of Jackson's loose tongue. When they were within sight of the infirmary, Harris called out softly for Nick. It probably woke Jordan too, but the fucker deserved it for not taking better care of Jackson.

Nick was waiting on the porch by the time they stumbled up to the house. He rushed forward to help Harris get Jackson up the stairs.

"What happened? Do I need to get Drew?"

"He's just exhausted. I don't think there's anything wrong with him that a good solid eight hours of sleep won't cure."

And maybe a meal or two. Jackson was a little gaunt.

There was no way they'd all make it up the stairs together, so Harris dropped back and let Nick pick Jackson up. Any other time the sight of Jackson being carried up a flight of stairs bridal style would have made him laugh, but the knowledge that Jackson would rather work himself to collapse than talk to Harris about what was bothering him made his stomach turn.

Had Jackson found out about the mate bond? That was the only thing that made any sense. Jackson had no reason to be angry with him—except for the huge secret Harris was keeping from him. He wanted to preserve their friendship, and telling your best friend they're your mate wasn't conducive to that. What if Jackson found out about the mate bond? What if he thought Harris was some kind of lovesick stalker who was just pretending to be his friend to get close to him?

"Tell Harry to go home," he heard Jackson whisper after Nick had gotten him to the guest room.

Harris's stomach sank.

"I'm going to finish the patrol," Harris answered.

"Never does what I want him to."

He heard a bitten off laugh that was probably Nick.

"No," Nick said solemnly. He closed the guest room door and appeared at the top of the stairs, giving Harris a long, pitying look. "I bet he doesn't."

"I'll check on him tomorrow, unless you think—"

"I think he's out of his mind with exhaustion and dealing with some personal things. He's not really mad at you, Harris. You don't have to worry."

"YOU'VE got the new security beacon?"

Harris held up the beacon. Jordan had ordered them a new set. The permanent beacons were keyed to a fingerprint. They used to keep them in the camp cars, but now they were on keychains. Easier to lose, but they wouldn't work for anyone but the owner of the beacon.

Anne Marie opened her mouth again, and Harris dug in his pocket and pulled out the laminated badge that had come in the same box as the beacons. It had an empty slot in the back that would fit a chip Candice carried to confirm Harris's identity. He was told it was standard protocol when dealing with the rich and easily kidnappable.

Harris bit back a chuckle when Anne Marie snapped her mouth shut. He'd never seen her so on edge about a camper's arrival before, and they'd had a Saudi prince here a few months ago.

"I have her itinerary and private number. I have the badge and the beacon, and I'm taking the nicest

SUV we have, which also happens to be the one with the darkest tint on the windows. We'll be back here by noon tomorrow."

She squeezed his shoulder and offered him a sharp smile. "Don't fuck this up. Text when she's off the plane and in your SUV. Make sure she follows the protocol Jordan gave her."

Harris resisted the urge to roll his eyes. "Will do. Trust me, I've got this, boss."

Anne Marie swatted at him and stalked off to terrorize some other staffer. Harris had already stashed his duffel in the SUV and checked out the keys, so he made his way down to the garage.

Harris wasn't worried about picking Candice up from the airport. It was spending the night at Jackson's that had his stomach tied up in knots.

They hadn't spoken since Harris had dragged him back to Drew's two nights ago. Jackson had left the next day.

It was killing Harris not to pick up the phone to call him, but the ball was in Jackson's court.

It didn't stop him from texting Jordan obsessively, but Jordan was uncharacteristically mum on the topic. He did tell Harris he had no idea why Jackson was mad.

Drew hadn't been any help either. He'd assured Harris that Jackson was physically fine, but he wouldn't weigh in on what was bothering him. He'd told Harris to leave it alone for a bit and let Jackson come to him.

Assuming Jackson ever spoke to him again.

This morning, Jordan had texted to confirm Harris was still planning to head over to Lexington for dinner and spend the night. Usually Jackson would be the one to do that. Harris was half-tempted to get a hotel out of spite, but that would complicate Candice's pickup

more than it already was. Jordan and Jackson needed
to accompany him to the airport as Candice's security
detail, so no matter how much he wanted to be petty, it
wasn't worth it.

He pulled out his phone and texted Jordan.

*Hitting the road early. Will be in Lexington
around 4, k?*

He could find someplace to kill time if they weren't
ready for him that early. Jackson's shifts at the station
were all over the place, but Jordan was usually around.
He operated Fang and Fury from the third bedroom in
their apartment.

His phone dinged as soon as he'd cleared the gate
on the drive out.

*NP, I'm out at a job site but Jackson's working
nights and will be home sleeping. Door's unlocked, just
let yourself in.*

Maybe that was why Jackson hadn't called. He
hated working night shifts because he spent his time
on stakeouts or filling in for beat cops. If he'd been
sleeping when Harris texted during the day, he was
probably annoyed with Harris for waking him.

He'd assumed they'd go out for dinner tonight,
but if Jackson had to head in to work, he wouldn't be
able to go with them. Harris could stop at a grocery
store and get something to make for dinner—he'd be
there early enough to have it done before Jackson had
to leave. It could be an apology for whatever the hell
he'd done to make his mate so miserable.

Harris huffed out a laugh. God, he was so gone
over Jackson. They weren't even in a relationship, and
he was cooking him apology meals after an imaginary
fight.

He was dialing Tate before he even thought about it. Harris was way overdue for a visit to New York.

Tate picked up on the fourth ring, just before Harris hung up.

"Harris, hey," he said, out of breath.

"Tell me I didn't interrupt you and Adrian having sex."

"You didn't interrupt me and Adrian having sex," Tate said dutifully.

Harris wrinkled his nose. "That wasn't convincing."

Tate laughed. "You really didn't. My phone was upstairs, and I was downstairs in the office. You're lucky I noticed it ring on my watch."

Tate lived and died by his smart watch. Harris was a bit jealous. Phones were a big no-no while seeing patients, but a watch could be discreetly checked.

"You're out of shape if a little sprint up the stairs made you breathe hard," Harris taunted. "You urban Pack types are lazy."

He'd gotten to run with the Connoll Pack when he'd been there for a full moon a few months ago. The Alpha maintained a cabin on a huge plot of land a few hours outside the city, and the entire Pack was welcome to run there whenever they liked. Still, it was nothing like living in the forest and getting to run at will. Tate and Adrian were getting soft.

"It's four flights, asshole. This lazy urban type runs about ten miles a day in Central Park."

Harris scoffed. "As a human."

"True. But you run as a human every day too."

"Because Drew's human, and it would be rude to leave him in my dust as a wolf." They'd gotten into a routine of sharing a morning run a few times a week. It gave them time to catch up. It was one of the highlights of Harris's day. Which was kind of sad now that he thought about it. "Besides, you have to run because you spend all day sitting. You don't even have a commute."

Tate and Adrian had spent what seemed like forever renovating their four-story brownstone. They'd had to wait out two leases, and the process itself took months, but the result was stunning. They converted the individual units into a spacious, comfortable house and used the bottom floor for Tate's practice.

"What's up?" Tate asked. "You didn't just call to tease me about my running habits."

He and Tate had been friends for years, and Harris told him everything, but this new distance between him and Jackson was different. Saying it out loud might make it real.

"I might have," Harris said.

"Spill." Tate was using his therapy voice, pitched deeper and no- nonsense. It was ridiculously effective.

"Jackson's mad at me," he blurted.

"Jackson spends half his life mad at you and Jordan for some idiotic thing you've done."

"But this time it's different. He isn't talking to me, and he never seems to want to be alone with me. I have no idea what's going on in his head, but it's almost like he's afraid of me. I don't know what to do."

Tate sighed. "Did you finally drop the mate bomb on him? That could take some time to process."

Tate had been advising him to talk with Jackson ever since he'd confessed that the crush he'd harbored for years on Jackson had turned into a one-sided mate bond. Harris had never taken the advice, and he didn't plan to. Jackson didn't want a mate, and Harris didn't want to alienate himself from his mate, even if they could only have a platonic relationship. An unrequited bond was better than a rejected bond.

"No. That's the thing. He just got, I don't know, weird."

Tate made a disappointed noise. "Then maybe it's time. What if he's feeling the bond, and he's confused? You can't just leave him hanging on this. It could be messing with his head."

Harris hadn't thought about it that way. What if Jackson *was* feeling the bond and didn't understand it? Maybe he was looking at this wrong. If he explained the bond, would Jackson accept it? Would Jackson still come back to Camp H.O.W.L. to visit? Or would Harris only see him in St. Louis for the holidays?

"Stop freaking out," Tate said, using his therapist voice again.

"I'll freak out if I want to," Harris said, aware how childish it sounded.

"If your bond is complete then Jackson could be feeling you freak out," Tate reminded him.

Shit, that was right. Why hadn't he thought of that? He was so used to living with the bond he hadn't even tried to tap into Jackson. If they had completed the bond then he'd be able to pick up on what Jackson was feeling.

"Is that like an instant thing?"

Tate chuckled. "I don't know."

"What kind of distance does that work over?" Harris chewed on his bottom lip, his chest tightening. He couldn't feel anything unusual.

"Depends. For me and Adrian? There's no limit. At least none we've found. I can still feel him even when he's in Portland. But I'm not sure what the typical range is for a bond."

Harris blew out a gusty breath. Adrian and Tate were moonmates, which was a different level of connection entirely. "Great. So I won't know for sure until I'm with him."

"Hey, it could be stress from work," Tate said, his voice gentle. "Jackson being distant might not have anything to do with you."

"You're right," Harris said. "I'm probably overreacting."

"That's not what I said. Your reaction is perfectly normal, but you're working without all of the facts. Take it slow, figure out what's going on, and go from there. Okay? Don't beat yourself up about this. You're in a difficult situation, Harris. That you've made it this long without going feral or breaking down is a real testament to your strength."

He'd heard of a handful of cases like theirs over the years. Mate bonds—both platonic and romantic— were common, but usually both sides acknowledged it. One-sided mate bonds were less common, but they did happen. It sucked that it was happening to him.

"If the bond is completing, that's a good thing, right?" Tate said after the silence dragged on.

"Sure. Of course."

Harris had spent the last few years hoping his bond with Jackson would complete, but now he wasn't so sure that was a good idea. What if it did and he got to experience that and then had it taken away? Enforcers couldn't have bonds of any kind. Not even a Pack.

Harris rubbed a hand over his face. What would he tell a wolfling in this situation? That it didn't do any good to borrow trouble. They always hated when he pulled that old chestnut out, and now he could see why. It was impossible not to worry about the future.

"Listen, I've got to go. Adrian and I are due over at the Alpha's for dinner tonight. I don't want to leave you hanging, though. Are you going to be okay?"

The obvious concern in Tate's voice made Harris crack a smile. "I'm good. Don't be late for Alpha Connoll."

"Text me later and tell me how it's going."

Tate worried like a mother hen, though he'd deny it if anyone called him on it.

"Will do."

Harris turned on music after he ended the call, determined not to let himself stew. He'd grab groceries and lose himself in cooking a meal for his mate. Taking care of Jackson always made him feel better.

Chapter Four

JACKSON knew Harris was in the apartment the moment he woke up. For starters, he felt more relaxed than he had in days. He could also smell Harris's scent over the spicy aroma of the chili he was cooking.

He groaned and pulled his quilt over his face. Harris was in his kitchen cooking. Life was so unfair. He'd hoped a few days apart would dull the need he felt, but it had only intensified it. He was going to have to come clean and tell Harris what was going on. Continuing to avoid him wasn't fair to Harris, and being a dick to him physically hurt. His wolf was going nuts.

He'd always been attracted to Harris, and he loved spending time with him. They were close, and he could see how that could morph into more. Not right now, though. Why couldn't this drive to mate have popped up later? Maybe in a few years when Jackson was secure in a Tribunal job and ready to look for a Pack where he could be Second.

He rolled onto his stomach and buried his head under the pillows. The thought of making a home with Harris had him hard in an instant. For a second he let himself pretend he lived in that future—that he was napping in their bed while Harris pulled together dinner in their kitchen.

Jackson rutted against the mattress, caught up in a fantasy amplified by having Harris so close. He'd given up trying to pretend that Harris wasn't his mate. It hadn't made the decision to ignore the mate bond any easier.

The shrill ring of the oven timer brought Jackson's hips to a sudden halt, reality streaming back in. He was hiding in his room while Harris cooked dinner. This wasn't their bedroom, and while he might acknowledge Harris was his mate, he wasn't *his*.

Jackson sighed and hauled himself out of bed. He'd grab a shower and get ready for work. With any luck, he could procrastinate until it was almost time to leave for his shift and then dash through the kitchen with the excuse of being late on his tongue.

Guilt seeped in while he was showering, and he sped up, steeling himself to man the fuck up and have dinner with Harris. The man was one of his best friends, and he deserved an explanation. God knew if the tables were turned, Jackson would be out of his mind with worry that something was seriously wrong.

HARRIS had the chili simmering on the stove and cornbread in the oven by the time Jackson wandered into the kitchen. Jackson had given himself the creepiest pep talk ever while he was dressing. He wasn't going to let his feelings get in the way of his friendship with Harris, and he would pretend the mate bond didn't exist. Couldn't be that hard, right?

Jackson's heart lurched at the hesitant smile Harris shot him when he walked into the kitchen. He'd been a terrible friend over the last week, and he needed to make it up to him. None of this was Harris's fault. Hell, none of it was Jackson's either, but he was the one acting like an ass.

Jackson perched on the counter, trying to summon a lightness he didn't feel.

Harris had unearthed a frilly apron Jordan bought as a joke and was wearing it over his jeans and T-shirt to save his clothes from chili spatter. He looked edible with his long sleeves pushed up to his elbows and a light flush across his cheeks.

"You didn't have to cook," Jackson said, picking up a handful of the cheese Harris had shredded and tossing it into his mouth to give his hands something to do. They itched to reach out and touch. "You're a guest."

Harris smacked his hand when he reached for more. "Leave some for the chili. And I'm hardly a guest. I invited myself over. Cooking for you was the least I could do."

Jackson nearly choked on his cheese. God, Harris was pushing all his buttons, and he didn't even know it.

He coughed a few times to cover the choking. "You're always welcome here."

Harris bent over to check the cornbread in the oven and Jackson thought his heart might burst out of his chest. He tried to look calm when Harris turned around, but from the way his eyes had widened in alarm, he knew he'd failed.

"These are done. Is Jordan going to be back soon?"

Jackson reached over him and opened the cabinet to grab two bowls. "He texted a bit ago. He's held up with a client and said not to wait for him."

Bastard. No doubt he'd texted rather than called because he knew Jackson would be able to hear the lie in his voice. Jordan was probably going through an Arby's drive-through right now and sitting in a parking lot until Jackson left for work. He'd also told Jackson to grow a pair and talk to Harris about what was happening, but Jackson wasn't planning to share that part of the message.

It was hard not to lean into Harris's warmth as the two of them moved around putting the finishing touches on dinner. It was painfully domestic, like a taste of what they could have if their bond was complete. Jackson didn't know whether to stockpile memories like this one to help get him through the bad times when his wolf cried for his mate or to do his best to forget them.

"Look, I'm sorry about how I've been acting," Jackson blurted as they sat down. "I'm not mad at you. I shouldn't have said that. It was never about you, not really. I was mad at myself, and I took it out on you. I've got a lot going on, and I'm letting it get to me."

Worry lines framed Harris's gorgeous dark eyes as he leaned in to listen, but he made no effort to interject. He just waited for Jackson to continue.

Jackson swallowed hard and steeled himself. "I really want the Tribunal job, but I'm realizing that if I get it, it's going to take me away from a lot of things I love."

Harris's expression eased and he sat back, nodding. "You've just gotten used to having Drew so close. It's going to be hard going back to only seeing him on holidays. I get it."

Jackson bit his tongue to keep himself from correcting him. Sure, he'd miss his stepbrother, but leaving him wouldn't be nearly as hard as leaving his mate.

Harris picked up the conversation, falling back into their old comfortable patterns. They chatted about benign things as they ate, and the anxiety that had lodged in Jackson's throat for the last few days eased. This was what he'd needed. He was an idiot for trying to avoid Harris.

Jackson gathered up their bowls, and Harris headed to the kitchen to find something to put the leftover chili in. He'd made plenty, and Jackson's wolf smugly crooned about this display of how well his mate could provide for him. Even after Jordan ate his portion tonight, there would be enough for a few more meals during the week.

Harris reached for the pot lid at the same time as Jackson, and Jackson found himself caged between the stove and Harris. He turned, heart stuttering, and came face-to-face with Harris. Harris's pupils dilated, and Jackson could hear Harris's pulse hammering almost as fast as his own.

Jackson gave in to his instincts and leaned in, hesitating a second as his lips hovered over Harris's. Harris was the one to close the tiny distance, and the first tentative touch of Harris's lips to his own set Jackson's nerve endings on fire. He gasped and leaned into the soft touch, letting Harris steer the kiss but giving as good as he got as it deepened. Harris ran a hand up his back, pulling him in closer, and Jackson wrapped his hands around Harris's waist, fisting the material of the thin T-shirt.

Harris kissed like a man starved for affection, and Jackson poured himself into it, meeting every nip and thrust with one of his own.

The sound of the front door slamming brought reality back with crystal clarity. Fuck, what was he doing? Jackson pulled away, unable to look Harris in the eye. He heard his mate breathing heavily and smelled how aroused he was, which made things worse. Jackson bolted down the hallway, tearing his uniform off as he went. He had to get Harris's scent off before he lost the willpower to walk away.

What would have happened if Jordan hadn't come home? Would he have let Harris fuck him on the kitchen counter?

Jesus.

He was fumbling with his belt when he heard a chair scraping across the kitchen floor, followed by Jordan whistling. What they'd been up to in there would be obvious to any Were with a nose. Even the spicy tang of the chili didn't mask the thick musk of arousal in the air.

Jordan cleared his throat. "Jackson finally—"

"Shut the fuck up, Jordan!" Jackson yelled from his bedroom.

"I'm going to go deal with that," Jordan said.

Harris had been quiet through the whole exchange, so Jackson had no idea what was happening. Was he horrified? Disgusted? Confused?

It almost hurt to breathe. Every inhalation brought Harris's scent with it.

Jackson was down to his boxers when Jordan pushed his door open and came in, mercifully closing it behind himself. The rooms weren't soundproofed, but it at least gave him some protection from Harris's scent wafting in.

"I'm going to finish putting this away and then go for a walk!" Harris called from the kitchen.

God. What if he hated him?

If he hadn't been so tuned in to him, Jackson would never have heard what he said softly to himself as he moved through the apartment. "Jackson finally *what*?" Harris mumbled. "Fuck."

Jackson held himself rigidly until he heard the click of the front door closing. He held his breath and strained, tracking Harris until the elevator doors closed.

As soon as he was sure Harris was out of hearing range, Jackson slumped onto his bed like his strings had been cut, panic welling up in his chest. Jordan was already going through his closet, finding another uniform for him.

"Dude," he said as he held it out to him. "Get yourself together. What the fuck happened in there? Harris looked like he'd been hit by a truck and then told his dog died, and you're in here looking like Leonardo DiCaprio in that freak-out scene in *The Aviator*."

"Fuck you," Jackson said, but the mental image made him chuckle anyway.

Jordan flashed him a grin. "Now that you're not staring at the door like it's going to eat you, wanna tell me what happened? I mean, I know *something* happened. The kitchen smells like a—"

"He made dinner, and he was just there being charming and irresistible, and I kissed him," Jackson said. He didn't want to know how Jordan thought the kitchen smelled.

"Okay?" Jordan said, drawing the word out into a question. When Jackson stayed silent, he added, "And did he kiss you back?"

Jackson squeezed his eyes shut. "Yes."

"And did you both seem to be enjoying yourselves?"

"Yes."

"And the problem is…?"

Jackson opened his eyes and shot an incredulous look at him. "The problem is with any luck I'm going to be in New York starting next month. A mate is a complication I can't afford right now."

"And yet you seem to have one," Jordan said, and Jackson hated how logical and calm he was being. Jordan of all people should understand. He didn't want anything serious right now either.

Jackson blew out a heavy breath and buttoned his shirt. His fingers trembled hard enough to make it a challenge, and after a moment Jordan batted his hand aside and did it for him.

"If you can't pull yourself together, I'm going to call in for you. You have no business being armed if you're this shaky."

That was the last thing Jackson wanted right now. He needed to get out of the apartment before Harris came back and demanded an explanation.

"I'll be fine. And if I'm not, they'll put me on desk duty for the night."

He hated paperwork, but concentrating on writing reports and updating case files would be a good distraction for him.

"Do you want me to talk to Harris?"

God, that would be even worse than when Jordan passed a note to Alexander Carmichael asking him if he liked Jackson in the seventh grade.

"Please don't."

Jordan gave him a long, serious look. "Okay, but if you don't talk to him about it soon, I'm going to do it anyway. And if he asks me any direct questions, I'm not going to lie."

The odds of Harris asking him if he was Jackson's mate were practically nil. "Fine."

IT was cowardly, but Jackson stayed at his desk filing reports long after his shift had ended. He'd spent his patrol shift at the front desk, taking reports from people who came in. His CO took one look at his clammy skin and shaking hands and threatened to put him on sick leave, but Jackson had pawned it off as a mild case of food poisoning and offered to work up front for the night.

He hadn't been able to stop thinking about their mingled scents and how right Harris looked puttering around in his kitchen.

Jackson hadn't been able to keep himself from leaning in and taking what he wanted, and now that he knew what Harris's lips tasted like and how he felt pressed against him, Jackson didn't know how he'd live without doing that every day.

Which was a problem. A big, complicated problem. Something had slotted into place last night when Harris was in his arms, and it scared the shit out of him. He didn't want a mate, but that's what Harris was. Someone he could count on to be there for him. Someone to run with under the full moon. Someone to build a life with.

But Harris's life was in Indiana, and Jackson's wasn't. Even if he didn't get the Enforcer job, he wouldn't be staying in Lexington forever. He wanted more for himself, more for his career. That didn't leave room for a relationship. He'd seen how mating changed people. His brothers had turned their lives upside down for their mates, and he was happy for them. He was. But that wasn't what he wanted. He couldn't be tied down by a mate right now. Not even one as perfect as Harris.

Jackson checked his watch and groaned. Candice's flight would land in less than an hour, so he had to pull up his big boy pants and go meet Jordan and Harris.

He'd turned off his phone when he'd gotten to work because he hadn't wanted to give in to the temptation to check it constantly to see if Harris had texted him. He dug it out of his pocket and turned it back on as he walked out to his car. Nothing from Harris, but several messages from Jordan and six from Drew.

He thumbed through them, tongue pressed against his teeth to keep himself from cursing out loud. Either Jordan or Harris had told Drew what was going on, since the messages from his stepbrother were a mix between asking if he was okay and berating him for hurting Harris.

He didn't need anyone else to make him feel guilty about it—he already hated himself for running away. But he still didn't know what to do about it.

Jordan's last message said Jackson could meet them at the airport instead of swinging by home first, which would save both time and the stress of being in the apartment together. Harris would be professional when Candice was with them, so Jackson planned to hide behind her like a shield today.

The airport was deserted when he pulled in. He flashed his Fang and Fury credentials to the attendant at the gate and drove up to the private runway where Candice's chartered jet would land. He parked next to the Camp H.O.W.L. SUV.

"She's running about an hour late," Jordan informed him when he got out. "There were issues with paparazzi stealing the flight plan, but they switched to a different airport and filed new plans."

"It gives us an opportunity to talk," Harris said, his expression neutral. It was his therapy face, and Jackson hated having it turned on him.

"I'm going to sit in Jackson's car and let you two hash this out."

Jordan disappeared before he could protest, so Jackson was left with one option. He stepped forward, sliding into the passenger seat when Harris opened the SUV door for him. He was relieved he hadn't opted for the back seat. With the center console between them, Jackson wouldn't be able to jump Harris again.

He stared straight ahead, watching a small Cessna land one runway over. Harris slipped into the car a second later, but Jackson kept his gaze focused on the plane.

"I owe you an apology," Harris said, surprising Jackson so much that he whipped his head around to look at him.

"What? No!"

"I do," Harris continued. He was looking at the steering wheel instead of making eye contact. "I—I'm attracted to you, Jackson, and I've tried my best over the years not to burden you with that. I value our friendship more than anything in this world, and I never want to jeopardize it."

Harris was getting this all wrong. The kiss had been Jackson's fault. If anyone should apologize, it was him.

"We were both in that kitchen. It wasn't just you."

Harris shook his head and looked at him. "I misread the signals. When you bolted, the only thing I could think about was how I'd ruined everything. I'd do anything to keep you in my life, Jackson. And if that means forgetting the kiss, then so be it."

This was exactly what Jackson had been hoping for, but the reality of it rang hollow. He didn't want to forget about a kiss so electric his lips buzzed for hours afterward. But he also didn't want the specter of that kiss and his attraction to Harris to crowd out their friendship.

"I think we can both agree that it was a mistake," he said carefully, ignoring the part of him that was screaming it wasn't. "And we still want to be friends. If we can move past it. You're one of my best friends. I can't lose that."

I can't lose you, he thought.

Harris's throat worked as he swallowed hard. "Yeah," he said, his voice breaking. "Yeah. Of course."

They both started when Jordan knocked on the window. Harris opened the door, and Jordan stuck his head in. He had a pair of gigantic neon noise-canceling headphones around his neck, and he held two pairs out to them.

"Candice's plane is early. Wheels down in ten minutes."

Harris rubbed his knuckles against his eyes, but Jackson wasn't sure if he was dashing away tears or just tired. He reached out and took one of the headsets.

"You should ride with Harris," he told Jordan. "I'll follow to make sure no one tails you."

They might have reached a tentative peace, but that didn't mean Jackson wanted to be in a car with Harris for two hours.

Harris nodded and blew out a breath. "T-minus ten minutes to teeny bopper. Roger that."

Jackson grabbed the headset Jordan held out for him and walked back to his car, thankful for the slight chill in the air. He pressed the side of his face against the cool glass, taking a minute to get his head back on straight.

"Go okay?" Jordan asked, popping up next to him. "I didn't listen in, but I did keep an eye out for bloodshed."

"No bloodshed," Jackson confirmed. "We agreed to forget about it."

Jordan let out an exasperated sigh. "You were supposed to talk about your feelings."

Jackson shot a hand out and twisted Jordan's nipple through his shirt, drawing a sharp squeak out of Jordan. "I'm feeling like you need to butt out," he said.

"Smitten you is vicious," Jordan said, rubbing his chest. "I like career-driven and lonely you better."

The plane Jackson assumed was carrying Candice banked overhead to come in for a landing, so he ignored Jordan's trolling, donned the headphones, and went to stand near the stairs that a man in a Day-Glo yellow vest had pushed out a moment ago. Harris paced by the SUV, and Jackson's heart broke. He wanted to go offer him comfort, but he was the reason Harris was so upset. It was a mess.

Jordan strode across the tarmac and wrapped an arm around Harris's shoulders, stopping him in the middle of a lap. The headphones didn't do much to dull the roar of the Cessna a few hundred feet away, Jackson had no chance of overhearing their conversation.

Jordan pulled back and nodded, offering Harris the smile that never failed to put their skittish clients at ease. He kept his arm locked around him, which Jackson's wolf didn't love, but at least he was comforting Harris.

The man with the stairs guided them over to the plane, and a minute later Candice appeared. She was in jeans and a T-shirt and had her hair up in a simple ponytail. From this distance, she looked like any other wolfling on their way to Camp H.O.W.L. Jackson hoped she got to have a normal experience there. He and Jordan had worked their asses off to give her the best chance. Now it was up to her and the wolflings in her cohort.

Chapter Five

"IF it really is her, then she *so* Photoshops her Insta. I mean, sure, filters, but c'mon."

Harris paused at the corner of the art studio, keeping himself hidden to eavesdrop on the conversation a group of wolflings were having.

"Like, she's totally had her boobs done."

"Omigod, what do you think will happen to them during the Turn? Like, will her body push them out?"

"Gross! Of course it won't, Trisha. Did you pay any attention in your Were biology sessions? Or is your Pack too poor to have those?"

All right, that was enough.

Harris steeled his expression into one of disappointment and strode around the corner, stopping in front of the small group of wolflings huddled over a phone. The trash talking continued until one of them noticed him, squeaking in alarm.

"I want all of you in my office, now."

"We have orientation in five minutes," one of the girls said. He zeroed in on her as the ringleader. She was the one who'd called another wolfling poor. These girls had been here less than a day—how had they already formed a social hierarchy? Teenagers were complicated.

"You will report to the director's office afterward, and she can give you a private orientation session."

The other three shrank into themselves, but their leader bristled and drew her shoulders back. The challenge in her gaze was clear.

"You can't make that decision. You're just the art teacher."

Harris frowned, then realized it looked like he'd come out of the art building. "Actually, I'm one of the counselors. But even if I was the art teacher, you'd still be expected to obey me."

She rolled her eyes. "I take it you don't know who my father is. He'll be hearing about how you spoke to me, and it will *not* go well for you."

Harris gritted his teeth and spared a moment to be grateful the majority of wolflings he worked with were decent kids. A little moody, but they were swimming in hormone soup right now, and that was before adding the stress of the Turn. But then there were kids like this little shit, wolflings who thought their Pack status afforded them special treatment.

He had a good guess who this wolfling was after her threat. The only true high-profile camper they had this month was Candice, but there were wolflings from a few prominent Were families attending. He'd dealt with an attitude exactly like this one a few years ago, and he'd recognized the last name when he was going over all his patient intake forms this afternoon.

"If you're Stephanie Chastain then I'm already well acquainted with your father," he said, amused when her expression turned thunderous. "Your brother Justin had quite a hard time adjusting to life here at camp. Henry and I chatted often."

Justin had been so terrible they'd been on the verge of kicking him out. Harris could count on one hand how many kids they'd expelled, but Justin almost joined their ranks. He'd disobeyed staff left and right and walked around camp with a huge chip on his shoulder. They'd drawn the line after his fourth fight. That had been around the time Jackson and Jordan moved to Lexington. After that cohort left Camp H.O.W.L., Harris and Tate, who'd been a counselor then, had driven over to their new place and spent an entire weekend drunk. That probably wouldn't be an option this time. Not after Jackson had kissed him. Harris had said he'd forget about it, but there was no chance in hell of that happening. The feel of Jackson's lips was seared into his memories. He could almost feel them now just thinking about them.

Which wasn't ideal, since he had a major situation to deal with. He wished Jackson were here. He was always better at playing bad cop than Harris was, and he needed to scare the ever-living shit out of these kids so they didn't cause even bigger problems.

He schooled his features into a disappointed frown. "I hope I won't have to call home with daily updates about you too."

She didn't have a retort for that, but she shrieked in outrage when he reached over and took her phone from her.

"Unlock it."

"No! What are you, some kind of fascist dictator?"

He gave her a grim smile. "I'm Tinker Bell compared to the director. You can either unlock it for me or you can unlock it for her. I guarantee you won't like what happens to you if it's the latter."

Her lower lip trembled as she tapped out her passcode. She had Candice's Instagram open, as he'd suspected.

"If you were going to orientation this evening, you'd learn that Kandie Bates is in your cohort. And she deserves as much respect and civility as everyone else. You will not post about her presence, you will not take any photos of her, and you will absolutely not harass her with your catty comments. Do I make myself clear?"

All of the girls nodded, and even Stephanie looked cowed.

"We're going back to my office to talk about how harmful gossip and bullying is, and then I'm going go over the same ground rules about Kandie's presence that the rest of your cohort will hear from the director."

Stephanie reached out expectantly, but Harris dropped her phone in his pocket. "You can have it back when you've proven you can be trusted with it."

"You can't just keep my phone. I'm an *adult*."

"I can and I will. The paperwork you signed before you arrived gave Camp H.O.W.L. permission to take the necessary measures to keep you and your fellow wolflings safe. If word got out that Kandie is here, you'd be jeopardizing the safety of everyone on campus."

Stephanie opened her mouth, but another girl grabbed her arm. "Shut up. You've already gotten us in enough trouble."

They walked across campus in stony silence. He ushered them into his office, giving one of them his desk chair and directing the others to the couch. When they'd settled, he perched on the edge of his desk.

"Do you understand why you're here?"

"Because you're a camp counselor on an ego trip?" Stephanie said, her expression downright hateful. "You know camp counselors aren't, like, actual counselors, right?"

Harris smirked and pointed over his shoulder at his framed diploma. "Oh, I'm sorry. I haven't properly introduced myself. I'm Dr. Wick, one of three licensed psychologists here at Camp H.O.W.L."

Stephanie deflated, but Harris wanted to nip this attitude in the bud while he still could. Tensions were high enough with Candice arriving and all the security changes—the staff didn't need a little stuck-up brat pushing their buttons right and left.

"Everyone here is an expert in their field. Our fencing instructor was a US Olympian and has a master's degree in kinesiology. Our archery instructor was also an Olympian, and she's still ranked seventh in the world. We take seriously our commitment to giving you the absolute best place to experience your Turn and learn to manage your wolf."

"And keeping us from orientation accomplishes that how?"

It was tempting to dismiss the other three and focus on Stephanie, since she was clearly the ringleader and the wolfling with the worst attitude. But taking the easy way out now would set up problems later. He almost laughed out loud at the thought—how much pain could he have saved himself if he'd applied that to his relationship with Jackson? If he'd told him about the mate bond when it formed then maybe they wouldn't be doing this awkward everything's fine farce.

"As I told you, the director will personally see to your orientation. I assure you it will be thorough, and you won't miss anything. What we're doing here is just as important."

"What *are* we doing here?" one of the other girls asked.

"We're going to discuss appropriate behavior, both on social media and in person," he said, and Stephanie rolled her eyes.

God, he was glad Nick was the one teaching the social media class this session. They traded off because it sucked so much. It was difficult to convince a room full of nineteen-year-olds that what they said and did online could have major consequences. And it wasn't just guarding against giving away their secret by snapchatting something that exposed wolves—it was also the basic human kindness aspect that seemed beyond almost all of their grasps.

Hell, even adults struggled with it. He'd had to learn Jackson was in a relationship with his last serious boyfriend, Raoul, on Facebook. That stung, and not only because Jackson was his mate. He'd done the same thing when they broke up—changed his relationship status.

Social media was brutal. Add werewolf puberty on top of that, and all the stress of the Turn, and they could end up in a disaster quickly.

"We're going to talk about why what you four were saying about Kandie's photos was hurtful. We do not tolerate bullying of any kind here at Camp H.O.W.L."

"I didn't even say anything, though," one girl said, tears welling in her eyes.

"You were all involved in that conversation. Even if you didn't say anything, by not putting a stop to it you're complicit. We have high standards for our campers here. We want you to leave Camp H.O.W.L. not only with solid control of your wolf but with a good grounding in being a respectful, productive member of society."

"Emma, you're not actually in any trouble. There's nothing he can do to us. Stop blubbering."

Harris handed a box of tissues to the crying girl. "I would usually call your Alpha at this point," he said, and that made Emma cry harder. The other two girls on the couch started sniffling too. "But since this is the first day and the incident happened before you got the camp's ground rules at orientation, I'm not going to."

They relaxed marginally, though Stephanie was still shooting him a murderous glare.

"One of the things the director is talking about right now is what H.O.W.L. stands for. Do any of you know?"

They all shook their heads.

"Honor. Obligation. Willpower. Loyalty. These are all principles that Were society relies on to keep everyone safe. We honor our Alphas, we obey our Pack rules and the overarching rules of the Tribunal because they are there to protect our secret. We have an obligation to help our Packmates, to look out for those who can't look out for themselves. Willpower, because it takes a lot of strength, both mental and physical, to keep the secret. One casual slip could damn our entire race, so we have to constantly guard against exposure. And loyalty, which is deeper than the Pack obligation to honor your Alpha. You'll make friends here this month you'll keep for your entire life.

"You shouldn't be tearing other people down to make yourselves feel better. It's a cheap thrill that doesn't last more than that moment for you, but your words can hurt someone for life. I don't want to hear about any of you bullying someone again, even if they're not there to hear what you're saying. If I do, you're out."

They normally gave the wolflings a longer leash, but with Candice on campus, they couldn't afford to give too many second chances. One good thing had come of this afternoon's fiasco. They'd been torn about whether or not to confiscate phones, and Stephanie's stunt proved they should.

He picked up his desk phone and called Scott, who was patrolling the grounds during orientation. The girls sat still, three panicked faces contrasted against Stephanie's pout. At least his message was getting through to most of them.

"Anne Marie is pissed you're not there," Scott said as soon as he picked up. "But since we're missing four wolflings, I figured shit had gone down or something. You do have them, right?"

"I do." Harris swept a gaze over the wolflings. "They're sitting tight in my office during orientation."

He held the phone away from his ear. "I'm going to finish this call in the hallway, and you're going to use the time to put together your most convincing argument about why the director shouldn't put you all on kitchen duty."

That was a bluff. Their chef would never allow wolflings in the kitchen. But they couldn't read chemosignals yet, so they wouldn't know that. He stepped out into the hall.

"Sorry, I wanted to put the fear of God in them before I left them. Tell Anne Marie we need to confiscate phones, tablets, and laptops. Cameras too if anyone brought one."

"Shit," Scott muttered. "Already?"

"They recognized her and had her Instagram pulled up and were making rude comments. If that's the worst of it, we're lucky. Let's shut all those avenues down before word of her being here gets out, if it isn't already."

"We've got the jammer Jordan brought up and running already. There's no cell service in the auditorium, and Anne Marie turned the Wi-Fi off as soon as Candice walked into the room. Your wolflings must have seen her on her way over. That was fast."

"That was *lucky*. We could already have blown everything. We should have had her stay in her room until after orientation. Fuck."

"It'll work out," Scott said, ever the peacemaker. "I'll talk to Anne Marie now, and we'll have staffers accompany the wolflings back to their bunks to collect all the devices. Did you have a plan for how to store them?"

There were seventeen wolflings this month, and at a luxury facility like Camp H.O.W.L. that meant upward of thirty devices. "There's a closet in Anne Marie's office that locks. I'll see if the kitchen has any bags and have staff members write the wolfling's record number on the bag with their stuff. We should write out receipts. No. Wait. Have them take a photo of the wolfling holding the devices. Between that and the number, we should be good."

"Parents are going to be pissed if they can't check in," Scott said.

"They aren't supposed to. We've been lax about that, but maybe it's time we start enforcing it. They can call home from the office phone if they need to, and parents can reach their kids through Anne Marie if need be. I'll talk to Anne Marie. Nick, Kenya, and I can call all the families tonight to let them know."

"Got it. I'll relay the message. You're keeping the wolflings?"

Harris grinned as the perfect punishment dawned on him. "I'm going to make them help."

THE mess was serving dinner by the time Harris and the wolflings had rounded up all the devices and stored them in Anne Marie's closet, so he gave them a temporary reprieve to go eat, with strict instructions to report back to Anne Marie's office afterward.

He'd woken Jackson from a nap when he called, which made sense considering he'd worked all night and then driven round-trip from Lexington to Camp H.O.W.L. His sleepy rasp had been painfully arousing, but Harris had a crisis to deal with, so it had been easier than usual to push that aside. Jackson hadn't been that worried, which was a good sign. Especially since they'd immediately put the crisis plan into action and confiscated all devices.

There was only one wolfling he hadn't stripped of electronics, and he knew she wasn't eating in the mess right now. He headed over to Drew's. They'd agreed Candice should lay low in social situations until she was comfortable merging with the other wolflings, and Drew and Nick offered to eat with her so she wasn't alone.

Drew left a plate out for Harris, and his stomach gurgled in gratitude as he slipped into the chair.

"How did orientation go?" he asked Candice before digging in.

She blushed and looked at her plate, unable to hold eye contact with him when she spoke. He'd written it off as her being tired this morning in the car, but as the day progressed, Harris realized she was shy. It was amazing how different she was from her confident, outgoing stage persona. Kandie wasn't fazed by anything, but Candice was a different story. She was quiet and curled in on herself like she was trying to take up as little space as possible. It was something he'd need to address in her therapy sessions, but tonight he just wanted to get to know her a bit.

"I feel really bad that everyone lost their phones because of me," she said, her eyes fixed on her mostly full plate.

That wouldn't do at all. She needed a lot of calories heading into the Turn tonight.

"First of all, you need to eat. Second of all, it's not your fault. We've actually had a policy that bans the use of electronic devices here for a few years, but we've only loosely enforced it. That's on us, not you. I imagine after your cohort moves on, we'll roll the device confiscation into our regular orientations."

"Maybe with something more organized than a pile of Ziploc bags," Nick said with a snicker.

"Hey, don't knock it. They are easy to label and can be sealed." Harris turned to Candice. "Speaking of, you're just another wolfling here. You're rooming here at the infirmary for now, at least until we can tell how well you can integrate with the other wolflings. But you're not exempted from the device ban."

Candice's jaw fell open, and she looked like every other wolfling he'd taken a phone from today. It was good to see her look like a normal teen. "I need it to talk to my agent and my publicist!"

Harris shook his head. "You're off duty for the month, Candice. It's very important you give both your body and your mind time to adjust. You can text Anne Marie's number to anyone who might need to contact you in an emergency, but you'd better warn them it has to be urgent."

She pursed her lips but dug into her sweatshirt pocket and came out with a bejeweled iPhone. "I'll tell them it has to be life or death," she said as she texted. When she was done, she handed the phone over to Harris, who left it sitting facedown on the table. It started to vibrate almost immediately, and Nick reached out and turned it off.

Candice slumped, looking more relaxed than she had since he'd picked her up. Eliminating her contact with the outside world had probably taken a huge load of responsibility off her shoulders. Good.

He nodded toward her plate. "When I said you need to eat, I meant it. Your body will use an insane number of calories tonight, and you need to have fuel for it to draw from. Trust me, you don't want to go into this dehydrated or malnourished. Let's give your body the best chance to move through the Turn easily, okay?"

Candice picked up her fork and Drew heaped an extra helping of chicken on her plate. They always served a carb- and protein-heavy meal before the Turn. A lot of wolflings would try to avoid eating, either because of nerves or because they didn't want to go into the most important night of their life with a full stomach. Staffers in the mess would be roaming around reminding kids to eat and passing out second and third helpings, like they were doing for Candice. Tonight's meal was chicken parmigiana.

"This is like, so weird," she said as she cut a small bite of chicken. "I haven't had carbs since I was a kid."

Harris shared a look with Nick and Drew over that.

"You're still a kid, kid," Nick said. He filled her water glass. "Hydration is just as important. I know we're annoying you, but you'll thank us tomorrow morning."

"I've been acting since I was six," she said matter-of-factly. "I had to start watching my weight when I was eight."

"After the Turn your werewolf metabolism will kick in. You shouldn't need to diet to stay in shape, and you'll definitely have to eat more than those bird bites you're taking. Even after the Turn, shifting takes a lot of energy. You're going to be putting on some muscle too, and that takes more calories to maintain," Drew said. "We'll talk about all this when you're in my werewolf health and biology classes, but I have a feeling it's going to affect your day-to-day eating habits much more than it will the other wolflings. If you've been dieting that long, I mean."

He furrowed his brow and pushed back from the table. "I'm actually going to go get some vitamins for you. If you've been malnourished for that long then you're likely calcium deficient and lacking some other nutrients that might make your Turn more painful. I've seen something similar before. Are you okay with shots? If I can give your vitamin levels a boost before the Turn, it should help a lot."

Candice looked horrified. "I'm not *malnourished*."

She was tiny and too thin. Harris thought there was a lot to Drew's theory.

"Look at it this way," Harris said, trying to placate her. "If you don't need the vitamins they won't hurt you. Right, Drew?"

"Right. In a human, I'd worry about the potential for overdosing someone if we hadn't checked their blood levels yet, but that's not going to be an issue for you, Candice. If there's an excess in your body, your werewolf metabolism will burn it off before it hurts you."

"Can I say no?"

The tentative tone in her voice made Harris want to punch something. There was some sort of abuse going on in Candice's background, whether overt or not. Someone had made her feel like she didn't have control over her own body and her own choices, that much was clear. From her uneasiness around other people and her shyness, he wondered if that same person had also made her think her talent was the only thing that anyone cared about. He'd never treated a child actor before, but he bet when he pulled journal articles on it he'd find similar attitudes and mannerisms among other child stars. They were going to have a lot to work on in their therapy sessions, and he made a mental note to start her out on daily sessions for the time being instead of the default three times a week.

"You absolutely have a choice," he said gently. "It's your body, Candice. You get autonomy over it. Here and everywhere else. We're here to help keep you safe and guide you through the Turn and the adjustment afterward, but no one will make you do anything you don't want to do with your body. That said, it sounds like the vitamins might be a big help tonight, and you should consider anything that can ease the shock and pain of the Turn."

"Healthy wolflings who have no vitamin deficiencies or other ailments go through the Turn faster than their peers who have health issues," Drew confirmed. "It's not going to be fun, but by making sure you're healthy, we can at least make sure it doesn't last too long."

The wolflings would start the Turn as soon as the moon rose. They'd lose themselves to it this first time, which Harris had always thought was part of the body's defense mechanism against pain. The Turn could be explained with the same clichés as childbirth—agonizing pain that's worth it in the end as it fades into a shadow of itself in memories. The wolflings would remember pain and confusion and the terrible rush of new inputs as their Were senses came online, but they wouldn't be able to give a play-by-play of the process a week later. It was a mercy, because the Turn was violent and painful. After that, shifting would be uncomfortable and take concentration, but they'd retain their full senses and selves while they were in wolf form.

"I guess we can do the shots," she said, pasting a smile on her face.

She took a bigger forkful of pasta this time, and Harris had to stop himself from praising her like he would a small child. She was a lot more innocent and trusting than he'd expected. Candice was one of the fastest-rising stars in Hollywood and by all rights should have an attitude like Stephanie's. Instead, she was much more like Emma. He'd have to introduce them. She and the rest of the girls—except Stephanie, who'd whined the whole time—had proven themselves to be hard workers and good kids. With someone like Candice rounding out their group instead of Stephanie, they could have an awesome camp experience.

"That was a mature choice," he said. "Eat up. We've got to start getting everyone downstairs into the Turn rooms in about an hour."

"I feel so weird," she said. "Like I have all this energy and no energy all at the same time."

"That's normal. Your body knows what to do. The hardest part is giving over to those instincts and not fighting it," Nick said. He offered her a reassuring smile. "We've all been there. And I promise it gets better. You'll feel the pull of the moon, of course, but it's nothing like the caged lightning of the Turn."

Harris had never heard it described that way, but it was spot-on. "I've got to get over to Anne Marie's office to deal with my troublemakers," he said, taking one last bite and standing up to put his plate in the sink.

The kitchen came equipped with a dishwasher, but Drew preferred to do them by hand, the weirdo. "Candice, we haven't gotten a chance to talk about this, but are you okay Turning in a group like the rest of the wolflings? We can set you up in a private room if you prefer, but your wolf will be happier if other wolflings are there."

She looked at him, wide-eyed and panicked. "Aren't we like, naked?"

Nick chuckled. "You are, but trust me, none of you will be in any frame of mind to notice. By the time morning rolls around, we'll have all of you covered with blankets, and when you shift back to human, there will be sweats for you to put on."

Most of the wolflings wouldn't have the control to shift back before moonset, so the staffers would be spending the night making sure the wolves didn't fight or get too restless in the Turning rooms. That rarely happened. Most of the wolflings were so strung out from the stress and pain of the Turn they ended up napping all evening. Harris usually brought a tablet to entertain himself, but tonight all the staffers were observing the electronics ban. He'd have to grab a book from the library on his way back from Anne Marie's office.

"I guess I can do it with the others," she said, but she sounded far from sure. "I mean, I have to get used to it at some point, right? I'm going to be in classes with them."

And in one of the cabins, if Harris had his way. He'd read her intake forms last night. She had no friends her own age and listed her agent and her publicist as her social circle. The kid needed a chance to be a kid, and this was the perfect place for it. He'd have to build up her confidence before throwing her to the wolves, literally and figuratively.

Chapter Six

JACKSON was nesting on the couch with his most comfortable blanket—not coincidentally the one Harris had used when he'd slept over—a bag of microwave popcorn, and Netflix when Jordan walked in and frowned at him.

"We've got to get you laid."

Jackson ignored him and turned up the volume.

"I'm not kidding, man, you're making everyone around you crazy. Ever since we got back from Camp H.O.W.L. you've been a moody little bitch." Jordan grabbed the popcorn bag and Jackson let him have it. He pulled a bag of Skittles out from underneath the blanket and ate those instead.

"Do you know your partner called me yesterday to ask if you'd had a death in the family or something?"

It felt like it. Mating was a stupid concept. He could kind of understand it hundreds of years ago when Weres needed to keep the population going to survive, but that wasn't a problem now. And even if it was, he was a dude who was into dudes. They weren't going to be popping out babies.

All the biological mating urge was accomplishing here was making him want to curl into a ball and whimper for his mate.

Stupid.

Jordan ripped the blanket away, and Jackson flung his hand out to grab it back, sending Skittles flying across the room. "Fuck you, leave me alone."

"I can't," Jordan said, shrugging. "This is coming from a place of love, Jackson. You need to stop sulking. Either accept that you're into Harris and go get a piece of that or come out and find someone to hook up with. You need to blow off steam before you end up wolfing out on a suspect."

He'd had a near miss yesterday, though he hadn't told Jordan about it. He'd almost called Harris, since he was second on Jackson's speed dial for a reason. They told each other everything. Except it was weird after the kiss and the agreement to forget about the kiss. Jackson sighed and pulled the blanket he'd wrested back over his eyes. He needed more time, and then all of this would go away.

He huffed out a breath when Jordan jumped over the back of the couch and landed hard on his chest. He wanted to scream at him, but he didn't have the breath.

"Either you're coming out to the bars tonight to find a little somethin' somethin' or I'm calling that fae prostitute you busted last year and hiring her for you."

Jackson shot up, dislodging Jordan and sending him sprawling to the floor.

"I will literally kill you if you call Dfearlie," he said, anger pumping through him. "Fuck you for even suggesting that. You know she was a victim of trafficking. She wasn't on the streets willingly. That bastard was feeding her iron supplements to keep her docile."

Jordan held his hands up. "Dude, I know. Besides, do you really think I'd risk the wrath of the Fae Council by propositioning one of the court? I just wanted to get you up."

Jackson's temples throbbed. "You can't joke about that shit."

He rubbed his face, surprised to find stubble there. Hadn't he just shaved this morning? He looked out the window, shocked to see it was pitch black. Had he been on the couch watching Netflix for that long?

"Seriously, though, the Fae Guard will fuck your shit up if they hear you say anything like that. You know they already monitor us because of Fang and Fury. You want to get on their bad side? They make Tribunal Enforcers look like preschool teachers."

He shuddered at the memory of finding a mutilated Were corpse a few years ago when Fang and Fury was new. They'd been working a missing persons case, and they'd found him—but only after the fae had finished with him. There was no concept of innocent until proven guilty among the fae. They were the top of the paranormal political food chain, and no one messed with them. For the most part, they let the other supernaturals govern themselves, but if they deemed someone a risk of exposure, they'd deal with it—brutally.

"Well, now that you're up, let's get you showered and dressed," Jordan said cheerfully.

Jackson sighed but let Jordan steer him down the hallway. Maybe he had a point. Jackson had been having a dry spell, so this attraction to Harris might be lust. That was easy enough to test by going out. And if it was, he could satisfy that with anyone and then be back to his normal self.

WHEN they arrived a Jordan's favorite club a little after eleven, the place was packed, which wasn't a huge surprise since it was Friday. Or was it Saturday? Jackson honestly had no idea. He got up and went to work, then came home and huddled up in his room or on the couch. He hadn't exactly had a booming social life lately.

"How about that one?" Jordan asked, voice pitched low so none of the humans would hear him. Not that he had to bother whispering. The bass was so loud the humans had to shout to hear each other, even the ones standing side by side.

Jackson followed his gaze to a tall, wiry blond. He looked fit and tan in his mesh shirt and skinny jeans, and when he saw Jackson looking, he flashed him a megawatt smile and winked. It did absolutely nothing for Jackson.

Jackson offered him a small smile and shook his head, earning an eye roll and hair flip from the guy.

"Ah," Jordan said, stroking his chin. "A brunet? I figured you'd want to get away from that, but you do have a type."

No one in the club held a candle to Harris. Jordan pointed out someone with the same dark hair and broad shoulders, with Harris's bone structure and skin tone. Looking at him made Jackson physically sick.

"You know, I think I'm going to go for the first one," he muttered. The twink looked nothing like Harris so there would be no confusing the two.

He wandered to the bar and ordered a double pour of Jameson and a can of the local microbrew the twink was drinking.

"You on the prowl tonight, cutie?" the bartender asked when he handed the drinks over.

Jackson flashed him a grin. "Might be."

The bartender had kind eyes that were the same shade as Harris's, and Jackson didn't protest when the man leaned across the bar and tucked a slip of paper into the pocket of Jackson's leather jacket.

"I get off at four if you haven't found anything that suits your fancy by then," the guy purred.

Jackson thanked him for the drinks and made his way back through the throng. The blond twink wasn't standing against the wall where he'd been a few minutes ago, but after weaving through the haphazardly placed tables, Jackson found him hovering on the edge of the dance floor, talking to Jordan.

The dick.

Jackson stalked up to them, fixing a murderous glare at Jordan before turning to the twink and offering him the beer.

"Your friend was just telling me you're a cop!" the guy yelled.

"I was explaining you're coming off a long shift and you're a little grumpy," Jordan said with a shit-eating grin. Raising his voice to yell like the others, he added, "This is Tim, he's—what is it you do again, Tim?"

"I'm the director of vibes for Ratr," Tim shouted. "It's a dating app where you can rate your dates with people and they get a rank."

That sounded appalling. "Like Yelp for dating?" he asked, incredulous.

Tim's eyes lit up. "Yes! Dude, we should totally use that in our marketing." He pulled out an iPhone and fired off a text.

Jordan was stifling a laugh, and Jackson wanted to kick him. Instead he took Tim by the crook of his arm and guided him farther from the dance floor so they could talk a little easier. Mercifully, Jordan didn't follow, disappearing in the opposite direction to find someone for himself.

"So, director of what? I didn't quite catch it," Jackson said, hoping he'd misheard.

"Vibes," Tim said, bobbing his head. "Like, I make sure employees are happy and help with hiring and company policies and benefits and shit."

"So you're in HR," Jackson said.

Tim rolled his eyes. "We try to avoid language like that. We're a very forward-thinking company."

God, this was a disaster. He gulped down the rest of his drink and watched as Tim chugged his beer. It smelled weird, and it was a challenge not to wrinkle his nose.

"Wanna head around back?" Tim asked, a twinkle in his eye. "I mean, we can keep talking and shit, but that's not what you're really here for, right?"

Jackson wondered if Tim came on this strong with everyone or if Jordan had told him Jackson was just looking for a quick hookup.

"Sure."

Tim wound an arm around his waist. Jackson flinched when Tim's hand came to rest against his ass, cupping him through his jeans. No small talk or foreplay, apparently. Which was usually right up Jackson's alley.

He couldn't help but compare the thrill of Harris brushing against him by accident to the complete lack of reaction he was having to Tim's hand on his ass.

Fuck. Don't think about Harris. That was the point of tonight, wasn't it? Right.

They made their way to the back of the club where there were dark alcoves. Some were curtained off, but the one Tim led him to was just a high-backed booth with no table. It was dark enough he wouldn't have been able to see much without his Were senses, so he supposed it was sufficiently secluded. Jackson had never been a prude, but he also couldn't afford to get arrested for public indecency.

"Are you sure you want to do this here?" he asked when Tim started unzipping Jackson's jeans.

Tim laughed, but his expression turned incredulous when he seemed to realize Jackson wasn't kidding.

"This is what you're here for, isn't it? I mean, you wanted a quick fuck. I'm not looking for anything other than an orgasm, man. If you're—"

"No! I'm not. Looking for anything more, I mean."

God. Did Tim think he was hesitating because he wanted to get to know him? That he was looking for a boyfriend or something?

Tim relaxed back against the pleather sofa and let his legs spread out. Jackson's eyes were drawn to the bulge he started to caress. Surely Tim had noticed he hadn't been the slightest bit hard when he'd been going for his zipper.

Sweat broke out along Jackson's upper lip and his stomach rolled. He had to get out of here.

"I need some air. I'm—I'm not feeling well. Sorry, man."

He didn't stop to see how Tim had taken the rejection; he just turned tail and sprinted down the dark hallway. He didn't stop until he was outside, puking in the parking lot.

There was no reason he shouldn't be back there getting off with Tim. The guy was gorgeous and willing. But even thinking about it made Jackson's stomach lurch again. His hands were shaking, and he realized tears were blurring his vision.

Jackson pulled out his phone blindly. He could call Jordan, but what if he was in one of the other alcoves? He had to get out of here, and he was in no shape to drive. Jackson hesitated over Harris's name and then skipped over him for the third person on his speed dial.

It only took two rings for Drew to pick up.

"What's wrong?" Drew rasped out, his voice muzzy with sleep.

Jackson winced when he realized it was almost one in the morning.

"Never mind," he said, guilt eating at him. "I didn't mean to wake you up. Sorry."

"Wait," Drew said, sounding clearer already. Jackson pictured him sitting up and turning on a light. He'd always done that when the hospital called in the middle of the night. He said it kept him from drifting back to sleep and helped his brain wake up. "What's going on? Are you hurt?"

Fuck, he was stupid. Of course his brother would think he was hurt. Families of police officers were always primed for a late-night call. God, he was so selfish.

"No, no. I'm not on shift tonight. I was at a bar and—never mind. It's fine. I'll call an Uber. Go back to sleep. Tell Nick I'm sorry."

There was no way Nick had slept through the phone ringing. Jackson had been so caught up in his own shit he hadn't thought about what time it was.

"I'm calling Jordan," Nick said in the background.

Jackson slid to the ground, his back against the brick wall of the club, burying his face in his knees. This was mortifying.

"Jordan is coming out to take you home. We'll meet you there."

As much as he'd love to see him right now, Jackson couldn't let Drew make the two-hour drive in the middle of the night just because of a booty call gone wrong.

"No. There's no reason for you to drive out here."

"You sound like you're halfway to a panic attack," Drew said, his tone sharp. "We're coming. Go home, shower off all the club smells, and wait for us. Jordan needs to know where you are. Are you still at the club?"

"I'm outside, around the back. In the alley."

A few seconds later, footsteps crunched over the gravel and broken glass that littered the alley, and Jordan appeared at the mouth of it, phone pressed to his ear and a worried expression on his face. His shirt was misbuttoned and his fly was unzipped. Perfect. Jackson had managed to cock block both of them.

"I'm here," Jordan said into the phone.

Jackson swallowed hard. His senses were seriously fucked. He couldn't concentrate enough to hear the other side of the conversation. He needed to get out of here. His wolf was freaking out at being so vulnerable.

"We'll see you soon," Drew said before the call ended.

Jordan walked over, held his hand out, and pulled Jackson to his feet. He dusted the gravel off Jackson's ass and led him around to the car, which was a few blocks from the alley.

Jackson's face burned with shame. It felt like
the time he'd gotten in over his head at a house party
and his father had to come get him. Except he wasn't
fifteen, and alcohol didn't affect him anymore. He
wasn't drunk. He was lovesick.

Scratch that. It felt worse.

Jordan bundled him into the car, taking so much
care Jackson wanted to yell at him. He kept his mouth
shut, knowing full well he was damn lucky Jordan
wasn't yelling at *him*. Jordan was the one who had the
right to be angry.

Jackson spoke up a few minutes into their drive
when Jordan turned in the opposite direction of home.

"Where are we going? I want to go to bed, Jordan."

"I told Nick it was stupid for them to come to us.
They both have responsibilities at camp tomorrow. We,
on the other hand, are off. You don't work again till
Sunday night, so we're going to them."

"Just take me home."

Jordan shook his head. "It's either take you to them
or have them come here, and all things considered,
taking you there is the lesser evil."

That meant seeing Harris. Jackson's chest seized.
"No! I'm fine. I'm being a drama queen."

Jordan looked over and flashed him a grin. "Ain't
no one disputing that, sweet thang," he drawled. His
expression turned serious, his gaze raking over Jackson
before he turned back to the road. "You need to talk this
out, man. And I love you, but I'm not the right person to
help you right now. You need Drew and Nick. So, I'm
taking you to them."

Jackson fell back against his seat. "You're having
an intervention?"

Jordan raised an eyebrow at him. "Your brother-in-law called me panicking and pulled me away from a perky little coed to go rescue you. Yes, we're having a motherfucking intervention. And there better be beer."

THERE was beer. The good stuff, not the asparagus-infused microbrew or whatever the shit Tim had been drinking at the club. Drew liked dark beer, and when Jackson saw the Dragon's Milk bottles on the table in the kitchen, he knew things were serious. It was a barrel-aged stout Drew hoarded like, well, a dragon. He and Nick drove all the way to the Costco in Louisville to stock up once a month because none of the local liquor stores carried it.

Drew stood up and hugged him hard when they walked in. Jackson melted into the embrace, burying his face in Drew's neck and breathing in the comforting scent of Pack.

"There are sweats upstairs in your rooms. Why don't you go shower off the bar, and we'll go out on the patio."

Oh fuck. Candice was staying at the infirmary. Had he woken her too? He glanced upstairs, worried, but Drew just chuckled.

"She moved over to a cabin a few days ago. There are some good eggs this month, and she fell in with a couple of them. Emma was one of the wolflings who got in trouble the first day, but since then she's been a model camper. She and a few other wolflings rallied around Candice and have been keeping her from the worst of the rumors and jokes going around campus. They're in Kayla's cabin."

Jackson let out of whoosh of breath in relief. So he'd only wildly inconvenienced Nick and Drew. And Jordan. And whoever was patrolling tonight and stationed at the gate.

Ugh.

"Shower," Nick said, pointing up the stairs. "You smell like beer and smoke and something weird."

"It's the beer," Jackson muttered as he left the kitchen. "Fucking hipster-shit vegetable beer."

Jackson showered quickly, relieved to scrub off Tim's scent. He'd been low-key nauseated the entire drive to Camp H.O.W.L., his stomach cramping every time he'd caught a whiff of it. The sweats Drew had left for him were Harris's. He felt instantly better when he pulled them on, cocooning himself in his mate's scent. The headache building behind his eyes dissipated, and his stomach calmed enough that the beer waiting for him downstairs actually sounded good. Though he was afraid to ask how Drew had gotten Harris's clothes. Had he gone over to Harris's cabin and borrowed them after Jackson had called? Did Harris just keep clothes stashed here?

That was probably it, he realized as he padded down the stairs. All the staffers kept clothes stashed in buildings around campus in case they had to shift unexpectedly. He'd bet there was a closet here in the infirmary with something from everyone.

He flicked a glance at his phone screen. He'd been tempted to text Harris on the way over to get all this off his chest, but he was glad he hadn't. That would have made things messier, even if it would have been a relief.

Jordan was sitting at the table, wet hair slicked behind his ears, but he grabbed his beer and stood when Jackson came in.

"This is a family thing," he explained as he headed for the stairs. "I'm going to finish this and get some sleep."

The clock on the microwave said it was almost four. Probably not a good time to be drinking. Then again, the alcohol didn't affect him, so there wasn't any reason *not* to drink a beer in the morning, and if his very human stepbrother didn't care—well, who was he to judge? Jackson shrugged and picked up the bottle Nick opened for him.

He followed Nick and Drew out to the porch, settling in a wicker rocker.

"What happened tonight, Jackson? We're worried about you."

Drew's voice was laced with concern, and Jackson's stomach churned with guilt. He'd been a real head case, and everyone had been walking on eggshells around him for weeks.

"Jordan convinced—" He stopped and shook his head. He was an adult. He made his own choices. "I went out to get laid and… I don't know. It didn't feel right?"

Drew raised a brow. "Are you asking me or telling me?"

Jackson shook his head. "It didn't feel right," he repeated. "But I got into it with a guy anyway, and once we started—" He swallowed back bile. "Nothing happened. We didn't even kiss, but just the *idea* of it made me sick. Like, literally. I puked in the parking lot."

Drew got up and put a hand against Jackson's forehead. "You're not warm. Maybe a little clammy. Do—"

Nick tugged him back to the couch they were sharing across from Jackson. "He's not sick, Drew."

Drew narrowed his eyes. "If he's throwing up—"

"Trust me, this is more my field than yours. And not just because he's a Were," Nick said, cutting off Drew's argument.

"Because it's psychological. My wolf," Jackson murmured, closing his eyes. "All I could think about was how this guy wasn't Harris. And even being there with him felt like a betrayal."

Drew sat back down, eyes wide. "Well."

Jackson leaned in, desperate. "Help me understand what's going on with Harris. I—I've never felt like this about anyone. It doesn't make any sense. I can't stop thinking about him, and not being with him is physically painful. I'm sleeping like crap, and my concentration is shot. I swear something snapped wide open in me when we kissed, and I can't put it back in its box, no matter how hard I try."

"What's to understand? You find him attractive. He finds you attractive. It's a tale as old as time."

Nick snorted out a laugh. "Which one is Belle? Probably Harris. Jackson's definitely a beast."

Jackson ignored his brother-in-law and focused on Drew. "I've always been attracted to him. Why now, though?"

"Well," Nick broke in again, a grin spreading across his face, "when a werewolf reaches a certain age, he starts getting tingly feelings in his—"

Drew elbowed him hard, cutting him off with a choke. "Don't be a dick."

Nick rubbed his ribs and laughed. "I'm always a dick. It's why you love me. Listen, Jackson, you're settling down. It's natural your wolf would look for a mate."

Jackson gaped at him. "I'm settling down? Really? I don't know if I've gotten my dream job or not, which,

I might add, would require me to move away from my family and join a new Pack. *That's* settling down?"

Drew leaned forward and squeezed Jackson's knee. "Kinda, yeah. I mean, you're moving from one phase of your life into another. It makes sense. You're getting more serious about your career and really starting to think about the future. Your instincts are driving you to find someone to share it with."

Jackson picked at the label on his bottle, unease sitting heavy in his chest. "So, my wolf wants a mate, and what, Harris was convenient? I feel this way about him because he was there? That's so messed up."

Drew groaned and buried his head in his hands. "No, dipshit. If it was based on proximity, you'd be mooning over Jordan. You're not harboring fantasies of sticking your dick in *him*, are you?"

Jackson recoiled so hard he almost dropped his bottle. Bits of shredded label floated to the floor. He looked up at the ceiling, praying Jordan hadn't heard that. "Oh my God. Why would you say that?"

"Because it's just as stupid as you saying you're falling in love with Harris because he was the nearest warm body. Jesus." Drew looked up, eyes blazing. "I swear, Jackson—brother or not, if you fuck him up we'll have words. I mean it. He has been in love with you for years, and I'm not going to let you hurt him. He's a good guy, Jackie, and he deserves a hell of a lot more than that."

The way Drew growled his childhood nickname made Jackson bristle more than the threat. Drew was the nice one—Jackson had never heard him sound so disappointed and angry.

"I'm not!" He took a breath and put down his bottle, leaning in so he was eye-level with Drew. His skin was itching with the need to shift and run. "I wouldn't. I'm just freaking out, Drew." His stepbrother's words finally sank in, and Jackson lost his breath. "Wait."

"Yes," Drew said, sounding equal parts exhausted and exasperated. "And I'm not telling you anything more about it because it's his to tell, but you're both fucking idiots."

Harris was in love with him? Jackson didn't know whether to be thrilled or terrified. He'd thought this was one-sided, and that made it easier to handle. If it was requited—fuck. That was so much harder. It would be easier to walk away from this if Harris wasn't involved.

Jackson gripped the edges of the chair, his claws threatening to pop as his skin prickled with the need to shift. "I don't know what to do. Tell me what to do."

The anger melted out of Drew's expression, and he reached out to rest a hand along Jackson's jaw. The warm, familiar touch calmed Jackson, and he closed his eyes as he took in a deep lungful of air, the scent of Pack grounding him.

Drew's hand fell away after a few seconds, and Jackson opened his eyes to find Drew and Nick looking at each other with dopey expressions. Their arousal and contentment clouded the air, making Jackson wrinkle his nose.

"How can you two flirt when my life is falling apart?"

"Because it's romantic," Nick said, his gaze moving over to Jackson.

Drew's followed a split second later, looking so lovestruck that Jackson was torn between jealousy and disgust.

"You couldn't get your head out of your ass until my brother almost died," Jackson pointed out. "You're hardly the epitome of romance. You two danced around each other for a ridiculously long time before admitting you had feelings for each other."

"Sound familiar?" Drew said dryly, drawing a choked laugh out of Nick.

"Fuck off," Jackson said, throwing a couch cushion at him. He was done talking about this with them. They were no help. "If you fucking shoot Harris to make a point, I'll gut you."

Nick's smile turned feral. "Gotta go through me."

Jackson scoffed. He held up his hand and shifted a single claw to flip Nick off. "Some challenge."

Nick and Drew erupted into laughter, and Jackson joined them a second later. It was a relief he still could. He felt lighter than he had in weeks as the three of them laughed so hard tears streamed down their faces.

"I'd forgotten you could do that," Drew said after they'd settled and reconvened in the kitchen with fresh beer. "God, do you remember that summer you learned? You drove everybody crazy. You were obsessed."

Jackson's cheeks ached from laughing, but he smiled anyway at the memory. "Dad can do it, and he said that kind of control over your shift is necessary if you want to be a Second."

Drew turned to Nick. "He spent hours every day shifting. Mom couldn't keep enough food in the house. God, I think she went to the store every other day that summer. She was so pissed."

"How old were you when you learned to do it? That's some serious control," Nick said. "I didn't even know that was possible."

"He was just a few months past the Turn."

Something inside Jackson preened at the pride in Drew's voice. He shrugged it off. "It's a skill I needed, so I acquired it."

"And that's why he's in the running for East Coast Tribunal Enforcer," Drew said, slapping Jackson on the back. "And also why he's never had a serious relationship, so he's totally freaked by finding his mate."

Jackson scowled at him. "I'm not—"

"You so are," Nick said, nodding.

Jackson sighed but didn't disagree again. They had a point.

"You need to be having this discussion with Harris," Drew said.

That was also true. But it wasn't something he was going to start before dawn. "I know. He's going to hate me."

Drew made a sympathetic sound. "He could never hate you. Are you positive you don't want to pursue the mating bond with him?"

Jackson nodded. "I can't be bonded to someone and be an Enforcer. It's a Tribunal law. I *can't*."

His wolf was tearing him up inside, but he ignored it. "I mean, I want to be with him. As boyfriends or whatever. But I can't mate with him. And I don't know what he wants, but it wouldn't be fair to lead him on if he wants a mate."

Drew nodded, eyes sad. "Why don't we all head up to bed? Maybe things will look different in the morning."

Sleep sounded divine. It wouldn't make his problems disappear, but at least he'd be thinking clearly. Jackson had slept more than usual over the last week, but it hadn't put a dent in his exhaustion. He made his way upstairs, resigned to spending the next few hours until sunrise tossing and turning, but as soon as his head hit the pillow he was out.

It seemed like seconds later when he opened his eyes, disoriented. His mind told him he'd just lain down, but the room was flooded with light, and he felt better than he had in days. The quilt on the bed had barely moved—he'd slept like a stone.

He curled up tighter, pulling the quilt up to his ears. His scent mingled with Harris's on the sheets and his sweats, which explained why he'd conked out so hard.

Jackson took a deep breath and forced himself to toss the quilt back and get out of bed. He brushed his teeth and rubbed at the two days of growth on his face. He could bother Drew for a clean razor, but he kind of liked this. He looked like a harder, more grizzled version of himself. The kind of guy who could look his mate in the face and tell him he couldn't complete the mating bond with him.

Jackson steeled himself and grabbed his phone off the nightstand. It was best to get this done as soon as possible. Just like ripping off a Band-Aid. His hands were shaking as he composed the text, but he sent it out without letting himself hesitate.

Hey. Can we talk? I haven't been honest with you. I'm here at camp. I'll meet you wherever, just tell me when and where.

Chapter Seven

HARRIS stared at his phone, his heart in his throat. Jackson's text had come through ten minutes ago, and he hadn't been able to make himself respond.

Jackson wanted to talk. And he was here. Did that mean he wanted to kiss him again? Or maybe it was the opposite. Maybe he'd driven all the way over here to tell Harris they couldn't be friends.

Sweat prickled across his back as he stared at the phone as if it were a cobra ready to strike. He'd thrown it on the bed after he'd read the message, like Jackson might materialize after he'd opened it.

He needed to get a hold of himself. Jesus.

He had mess duty this morning, and a few sessions this afternoon, but most of his day was free. Harris left the phone on the bed as he finished getting ready, grabbing it as he swept out the door. He was late, and depending on who else drew Sunday morning mess monitoring, he might be in deep shit.

Harris's stomach swooped as he took out his phone and shot off an answer.

Boathouse at 11? I'll bring an early lunch for us.

He'd assume good news. That was what all the empowerment gurus said to do, wasn't it? Visualize the outcome you desire and all that jazz. Harris turned off his phone so he wouldn't be tempted to check it while he was on duty and pulled open the door of the mess, bracing himself for a tirade if his partner for the morning was Kenya or Richard.

A weight lifted off his shoulders when he saw Kayla hovering over by the waffle bar. She probably hadn't even noticed he was late, and if she had, she wouldn't care. She might be the tiniest staff member, but she was by far one of the scariest. He'd seen six-foot wolflings reduced to tears when she marched them out of a room by their ear.

The mess was still deserted, which wasn't a surprise. Sundays were low-key, a few fitness classes in the afternoon and lots of rec time built in. The mess opened at nine and served brunch until eleven, and wolflings trickled in and out as they woke up for the day. It was a far cry from the usual hectic bustle of mealtime at Camp H.O.W.L., and Harris didn't know whether to be grateful because it gave him time to think or not. He'd have been better off with a lunch rush where he was too busy breaking up potential food fights and mediating disagreements.

"What's got you ruffled?" Kayla asked when he joined her in front of the syrups.

"Jackson's here, and he told me he wanted to talk," he said, sliding a hand into his pocket to run over the hard edge of his phone.

"Like talk or *talk*," she said, doing something with her eyebrows that made Harris wince and take a step away. "Everybody knows you two are one smoldering look away from boning. The UST was actually painful while he was here a few weeks ago."

"Can you speak English instead of Tumblr for once? What the hell is UST?"

Kayla laughed. "Unresolved sexual tension. And you two have it in spades. Plus your boy has no game."

That wasn't true. He'd watched Jackson charm countless guys in clubs. He had game; he just didn't use it with Harris. Was that a good thing or not?

"I don't know. I'm hoping it means he's interested, but who knows. I mean, we've known each other for how long, and he's never once looked my way. Why now?"

She shrugged and put the top on a syrup bottle. "He could say the same thing about you, couldn't he?"

That was true. Was it possible Jackson had been harboring feelings for him all this time and hadn't said anything? He'd always smelled of lust when they were together, but that was Jackson. He'd never given the slightest indication it was anything other than appreciation for a fit male specimen. Harris wasn't going to pretend modesty here. He was in top shape and took care of himself. He was a catch.

Kayla dashed away to stop two wolflings from coming to blows over whether or not ketchup belonged on eggs, and Harris walked an aimless trail through the mess, weaving in and out of tables and keeping an eye out for shenanigans. Sundays were the only days the wolflings were allowed to sleep in, so most of the troublemakers weren't up yet. He stopped by Candice's table, pleased to see her eating with Emma and a few other wolflings.

The two weeks she'd spent here already had done wonders for her. She looked healthier, her color was great, and best of all, she was smiling and eating without hesitation. She looked like any other wolfling. It was a far cry from the way she'd picked at her food when she'd arrived, scared of putting on weight.

He pulled a chair out and spun it around, sitting in it backward so he could lean in toward the table. "What are you guys up to today?"

Emma lit up. "We're going to swim out to the floating dock after classes this morning. Hannah said she heard there were selkies in the lake, so we're going to see if any of them come out."

There weren't any selkies in the lake. A naiad dropped in every month or two to check on the quality of the water and the health of the fish, but that was the only supernatural creature that had ever set foot—or fin—in it aside from Weres here at the camp. The camp's borders were off-limits. No one entered their territory without permission. The naiads and dryads always called ahead first, and the fae gave the camp a wide berth. It had been years since the camp had any trouble.

"Sounds fun," he said, sharing a grin with Kayla, who was across the room. "Don't forget we've got a midnight hike coming up this week and the tracking challenge too. You might want to go for a run and try to test your noses after your swim."

They nodded excitedly, all five of them chattering about things they'd heard about the special activities. Wolflings who'd had older siblings at the camp often came already expecting the late-night activities and special challenges, and those who didn't found out about them within the first week. "Keep that to yourselves," he added quietly, tapping his lips with his finger.

Anyone in the mess could easily hear him, which was another reason counselors gave out hints about upcoming activities like this. It taught the wolflings to always be aware of their surroundings.

Candice looked up at him, a wide smile splitting her face. "Can you give me some advice about the tracking challenge during my session today? Our cabin wants to be ready. The boys in cabin three have been trash-talking and saying they've got it all wrapped up, and we want to teach them a lesson."

He winked. "We'll see."

She'd made big strides in therapy too. Her body had been racked by the Turn longer than the other wolflings in her group, but she'd borne it in silence, not looking to the others for support. When the rest of the wolflings had curled into a big pile and napped, she'd paced the room, eyes wide and heart racing. It made his heart happy to see her thick as thieves with the other girls and not backing down from a challenge from another cabin.

More kids trickled into the mess, and he got up and made his rounds again, chatting with other wolflings and offering stern rebukes when things started to get out of hand or pampered wolflings left a mess. Everyone pitched in to clear trays, no matter how wealthy or important their families were. This far into the month, it only took a few sharp words to rectify most problems.

When things were winding down toward the end of brunch, he snuck back to the kitchen and asked Frank to make him a picnic lunch for two.

"You've got to give me more," the chef said, hands on his hips. "Are we talking PowerBars in a rucksack? Cheese and crackers? Strawberries and wine?"

Harris flushed.

"Ah, it's that kind of picnic. Say no more. I'll have it ready for you as soon as brunch service is over."

"No wine," Harris said quickly. "Maybe something between sandwiches and strawberries? Easy to eat, not too messy, but not too sexy either."

Frank grinned. "I got you."

Harris wasn't sure he did, but he left the kitchen anyway to check in with the stragglers and hurry them along, since brunch was almost over.

By the time he'd cleared the mess and made it back to the kitchen, Frank had a wicker picnic basket waiting on the counter. Harris tried to peek inside, but Frank batted his hands away. "Don't mess up my presentation. Just take it."

Harris rolled his eyes but took the basket. "Thanks, Frank."

"Thank me afterward," Frank said, making Harris's cheeks heat again. He headed for the back door. "Don't forget to take a blanket! Something thick and luxe."

Harris saluted over his shoulder. He had a cashmere throw he'd gotten as a gift from a grateful wolfling's family last year. He'd flown across the country with them when the wolfling had to leave camp, and he'd spent several days at their Pack compound helping the kid adjust to being home. The blanket was probably worth more than everything else in his cabin, but he never used it. He'd feel ridiculous with something that expensive on his bed. It would be perfect for this, though.

Jackson was already at the boathouse when Harris walked up. He had his hands in his pockets, and he was staring out at the lake. The raft in the center was empty, since the wolflings were all in their late-morning sessions.

He turned when Harris's feet hit the dock.

"Hey. Thanks for meeting me," he said. He looked stressed and tired, and Harris's stomach dropped.

"No problem. I didn't know you were coming up," he said, unlocking the door to the boathouse and letting Jackson walk in first. They kept it locked to deter randy wolflings from using it as a hookup spot, an irony that was not lost on Harris as he spread his blanket out on the cedar-plank floor and opened the picnic basket.

"It wasn't planned," Jackson said. He rubbed the back of his neck, looking sheepish. "I went out last night, and things got out of hand. Jordan drove us up in the middle of the night."

There weren't many ways things could get out of hand for a Were. They couldn't get drunk, and he knew Jackson wouldn't mess with illegal drugs. He bit back a million questions and waited for Jackson to continue.

"I was with a guy last night. At a club."

Harris looked away and busied himself with unpacking the picnic. He'd been an idiot.

"No," Jackson said, kneeling on the blanket next to him and stilling his hands with his own. "I mean, I tried. Because all I've been able to think about since our kiss is you. And I thought maybe I could get you out of my system. But I couldn't. I *didn't*."

Harris sat back on his heels, shaking Jackson's grip off. "I don't know how you expect me to react here," he said, hurt coursing through him. "I—I know we said we'd forget about the kiss and just be friends, but I don't want to hear about your hookups, Jackson. I can't be that kind of friend for you right now."

"Fuck," Jackson said, pressing the heel of his hand to his eyes. "This is coming out all wrong. I didn't do anything with the guy, Harry. Just being there with him felt wrong when it was you I wanted to be with. I left him sitting there and went outside and called Drew, and the next thing I know Jordan is picking me up off the ground and bringing me here."

Picking him up off the ground? Harris sat up on his knees and put his hands on Jackson's shoulders, looking him over. He didn't look injured, and Harris hadn't smelled anything but anxiety on him. "What happened? Why were you on the ground?"

Jackson grabbed his hands. "Because my wolf was going nuts. I thought I was going to lose it in that alley. I—I can't sleep, I'm snappy with everyone. I don't want to keep ignoring what I feel for you."

Harris didn't know what to say, and he didn't think he could get the words out even if he did. His heart was in his throat. Jackson wanted to be with him? After years of waiting, could he really be here with his mate, listening to him say he wanted to be together?

"I mean, you know this has an expiration date. Even if I don't get this job with the Tribunal, I'll get one eventually. It's the next logical step for me. But there's no reason we can't be happy for now, right?"

Harris's chest seized, Jackson's casual words crushing all the air out of his lungs. He swallowed back bile and pasted a smile on his face. Was having a limited time with his mate better than never having him at all?

Jackson stared at him, expression worried. Harris needed to say something soon or he'd lose him for good this time. His scent was already turning from nervous and hopeful to the bitter tang of sadness and rejection.

"Of course," Harris rasped out. "Of course I want to be with you for however long I can have you."

Jackson's eyes lit up, and he cupped Harris's face with his palms. "I want to do this the right way," he said. "No running away after, I promise."

No staying either. But that was something Harris could deal with later. He didn't have the strength to deny his mate anything, especially this.

He mirrored Jackson's pose, cupping his face reverently. Harris couldn't believe he was allowed to touch. Stubble pricked against his palms, as good as a pinch to assure him this was really happening. He leaned forward and pressed a soft, chaste kiss to Jackson's lips.

It was over almost as soon as it began, and Harris pulled away with a smile. He needed time to process this and prepare himself before they went any further. He was going to come out of this heartbroken, but it would be more than worth it. Still, he had to do what he could to protect himself, and giving himself to Jackson when he was this flayed open and vulnerable would be a mistake he'd regret for the rest of his life.

"I've been waiting for this for a long time," he admitted. "But it's not going to happen in a public boathouse where anyone can interrupt us."

Jackson laughed and settled back on the blanket. "Fair. Should we eat? What did you bring?"

Grateful for a distraction, Harris busied himself with unpacking the goodies Frank had given them. "Actually, I don't know. I didn't pack it."

He pulled out carefully packed Tupperware containers of pesto caprese slathered on toasted baguette slices, briny olives, thick slabs of manchego cheese topped with quince paste, prosciutto rolled around tangy goat cheese, and figs dipped in honey sprinkled with walnuts.

True to his word, Frank hadn't packed wine. A bottle of sparkling pink french lemonade had been nestled inside with two glasses. It was perfectly chilled, condensation budding along the glasses as soon as Harris lifted it out of the basket and poured some for them each.

Jackson whistled at the spread. "I always forget how well you guys eat here. Makes me wish I could live here too."

You could, Harris wanted to say. Anne Marie would hire him in a heartbeat. He got along with all the staff already, and having a highly trained security expert on site would be a huge feather in Camp H.O.W.L.'s hat. But Jackson would be miserable here. He wouldn't make it a month before he went stir crazy. They helped people here, but it wasn't the help he was hardwired to give. Jackson needed to be out in the thick of things, putting his life on the line to serve others. It was who he was.

Harris let the moment pass and leaned back on his elbow, popping a fig in his mouth. He'd just promised Jackson he could do casual, and he wasn't going to start by nagging him to give up all his dreams and come live at Camp H.O.W.L.

"Are you staying all day? I have sessions this afternoon, but I'm free after four." Heat crept up his neck and spilled onto his cheeks. That didn't sound too much like a proposition, did it? He was up for that, of course. God, was he up for that. But if Jackson wanted to take things slow and just hang out, that was fine too. He'd take time with his mate any way he could get it.

Jackson swallowed his bite of prosciutto and goat cheese, groaning softly over it. "This is so good," he murmured. He licked his lips, and Harris had to force himself to look away. "I came with Jordan so I'll have to check with him, but I think we'd planned to stay the day. We'll head back tonight. I'm not on shift until Monday evening, but I doubt Jordan would agree to stay another night."

Harris's wolf wanted to whine at the thought of Jackson going back so soon, but it made sense. He had a life in Lexington, and after he got the Enforcer job, he'd have a life even farther away in New York. Logically, the short-term arrangement Jackson had proposed made sense. It was too bad Harris's inner wolf wasn't much for logic.

Jackson scooted closer, their thighs touching. "I want to kiss you again."

Harris's blood surged. "I want you to."

A feral grin split Jackson's face. Harris had a moment to wonder if he should have insisted they wait until they were back at his cabin before he gave himself over to the hot, insistent pressure of Jackson's lips.

Harris's muscles went weak, and his arm crumpled, sending them tumbling down. Jackson didn't break the kiss, bracing himself on his forearms so he didn't crush Harris but still pursuing his mouth like a hungry wolf after quick-footed prey. Harris brought his hands up and ran them over Jackson's biceps, gratified to feel them shaking. The knowledge that Jackson was as shaken by this as he was gave Harris confidence. He took control of the kiss and urged Jackson to lower himself until they were pressed together from chest to thighs. The weight of him was solid and reassuring. Nothing had ever felt as right as this moment, being pinned to the floor of the boathouse by his mate's body, limbs intertwined and mouths pressed together.

They rolled to the side, knocking over the lemonade. The bottle clinked against the planks and rolled away, the sticky liquid soaking into their shirts. Harris pulled away and laughed, then rested his head on Jackson's chest. Jackson's pulse was rabbit quick. When Harris pressed his mouth there, it fluttered against his lips.

Jackson wiggled his arm between them, grimacing at the mess the lemonade had made of his arm. "This is some Nicholas Sparks shit right here," he said, drawing another laugh out of Harris.

"I doubt any characters in his books would have crushed their romantic picnic rolling around like teenagers," he said, sitting up and picking a walnut off the back of Jackson's shirt.

"Whatever, you love it."

He did. God help him, he did. And he would be devastated when it was over. But that was a problem for another time. Right now, he wanted to get Jackson in his bed. And maybe his shower. They were both covered in lemonade, and Jackson had honey on his elbow.

Jackson had just leaned in for another kiss when the camp loudspeakers broadcast a high-pitched hum. It took Harris a few seconds to wrap his brain around it.

"Fuck!" He pulled away, looking around wildly.

Jackson seemed to process the alarm tones a few seconds later. He sprang up, grabbing his phone out of his pocket.

"Breach," he said, flicking his gaze up to Harris, who had pulled his own phone out.

He'd forgotten to turn it back on. Shit. His fingers were shaking as he fumbled with the buttons, urging it to boot faster.

"Far outer fence, quadrant six," Jackson said. His fingers were flying over the keyboard, probably firing off instructions to all the staff.

Harris took a breath and swallowed back the surprise and panic. He'd only heard the alarm tones during tests. They were high-pitched enough that humans wouldn't be able to detect them, giving the staff a head start on getting the wolflings to safety before alerting the humans they knew about the breach.

"I've got to go clear the buildings," he barked out.

Protocol called for the camp's three counselors to take charge of the bunker where the wolflings would hide. Kenya would already be there, opening the secret entry in the infirmary and guiding the wolflings who trickled in down to the safest place on campus. All the instructors would already be ushering their wolflings to the infirmary before reporting to their patrol positions. Kenya would take roll, and he and Nick needed to be in contact to see who was missing and find them.

His phone chirped, and he looked at it, breathing a sigh of relief. Sunday afternoon classes were mandatory. All wolflings had been with an instructor, and everyone was already in the bunker or en route.

"I'm heading to the back fence," Jackson said, ripping off his sticky shirt. "Take care of yourself, Harry. Get to the bunker. I'll text as soon as we have an all clear."

Harris had locked the door behind them so they wouldn't be interrupted, and Jackson fumbled at the latch with clawed fingers for a moment before getting it open.

As soon as he was outside, Jackson shifted and hit the ground on four paws, leaning in to a sprint as he took off around the lake. Harris kept his phone out in case there were any other updates but ran for the infirmary. He nodded to the staffers he passed, all of them heading to checkpoints and preassigned stations around the camp.

Nick was waiting for him at the top of the stairs. Together they carefully placed the panel back in place and lowered the security bar. The seams were undetectable from outside.

"Any idea what the breach is?" he asked, out of breath as they hurried down the stairs.

"None," Nick said, looking as shell-shocked as Harris felt.

Harris picked up speed when he heard shouting in the bunker. The hidden lower part of the infirmary was full of reinforced underground rooms the wolflings used for their Turn, but it also had a cement panic room that could fit the entire camp if need be. They used it as a place to gather and have breakfast the morning after the Turn.

"This never happens," he heard someone growl. "Not before *you* came."

"It could be a drill," someone else chimed in.

"At noon on a Sunday?" the first person scoffed. "Right."

"Hey now." Harris recognized Richard's voice. "I can't say I understand her life choices, but—"

Harris burst into the room, anger simmering under his skin. "Richard," he barked, "why aren't you in your quadrant? We need everyone out there in their assigned places."

He took in the scene in the room. A quick count showed all seventeen wolflings were present, and Kenya was hunched in the corner talking one through a panic attack. That's right. They had a camper who was claustrophobic this year. He'd gone through his

Turn in the infirmary with Drew and Nick because he hadn't been able to relax downstairs. This had to be a nightmare for him.

"Richard?" he prompted when the other man hadn't moved.

"I'm not risking my life because some little Hollywood slut exposed us all by coming here," he hissed.

Harris's gaze flicked to Candice, who had flinched at Richard's quiet words. Nick moved toward them, face like a thundercloud.

"I've got this," Harris muttered. "Start getting them calmed down, explain what we know. Last I heard the intruder hadn't breached the second or third fences. Everyone should be fine. This is just a precaution."

Harris shot Candice what he hoped was a reassuring smile and grabbed Richard by the shoulder, pushing him hard until he stopped resisting and willingly walked up the stairs. The bunker door required a code to open, and Harris leaned around him and punched it in, not bothering to conceal his fury now that his back was to the room.

He pushed Richard through the door and slammed it behind them, making sure the hidden panel had slid into place before he released Richard and shoved him hard against it.

"What the ever-loving fuck was that?" he asked, seething. "First of all, speaking about a camper like that is *never* okay. She's just a kid, Richard, fuck. And second of all, you are a member of this staff. If you want to remain a member of this staff, you will get your ass out there and patrol your section."

Richard's eyes flashed amber and he fisted his hands at his sides, hair sprouting along the backs of them. "It's ridiculous the way everyone here bends over backward for that little bitch," he spat out. "It's our duty to keep the wolflings safe, all of them. And we can't do that with her here. We're sacrificing all their lives for the sake of one selfish little girl who risks exposing werewolves every time she makes another movie or goes on another talk show. How long before something scares her on set and she shifts? Hmm? How many TV interviews do you think she'll do before she accidentally flashes her eyes? Her parents should never have let her go into acting, and you're deluding yourself if you think we're not signing our own death warrants by letting her continue to do it."

Harris fired a text off to Anne Marie. There was no way she would keep Richard on staff after this. He grimaced when her response came seconds later.

"You're done here, Richard," he said quietly.

Richard reached for the mechanism to detach the panel, but Harris was quicker. He twisted his arm and frog-marched him out to the porch.

"What the hell, Harris? There's an active threat on the grounds right now!"

"The intruder has been caught. Anne Marie said she's being taken to the security office. As soon as she's secured, we'll get the all clear to let the wolflings out."

Richard's stiff stance eased, and he stopped pushing back against Harris. "Then I'll—"

"You'll go wait for Anne Marie in her office," Harris said flatly. "I meant it when I said you're done here. You've proven yourself a coward and a bully, and we don't tolerate either at Camp H.O.W.L."

Richard's jaw dropped. "You don't have the authority to fire me."

Actually, he did. He was Anne Marie's deputy director. He could do whatever was necessary to keep the camp safe, and as far as he was concerned, Richard humiliating a wolfling in front of her entire cohort was ample reason to fire him. His refusal to follow security protocols left part of the camp unprotected, which was just as bad.

Anne Marie would have the honor of getting him off the grounds. Harris had to get back in there and make sure Candice was okay.

Chapter Eight

HARRIS was arguing on the porch with a staffer Jackson didn't know when he and Jordan walked by with the intruder held between them. Her wrists were bound with an industrial zip tie.

Jackson hadn't expected to find a selkie when he'd rushed out to the scene of the breach. Scott and Jordan got there first, and they had her subdued by the time Jackson ran up. Their protocols were aimed at human intruders, not other supernaturals. The werewolf camps were well known among the supernatural community, and everyone steered clear. The Tribunal took a harsh stance toward anyone interfering with wolflings. Werewolves gave the same courtesy to other supernatural communities—you didn't mess with anyone's children. Period.

There wasn't much infighting among the different supernatural groups. They were solitary and stuck to their own communities. Not many could pass in human society like Weres could, which was a point of contention. But today's break-in hadn't been about jealousy or resentment—it had been about greed, pure and simple.

"Selkie," Jackson mouthed when Harris caught his eye.

Harris craned his neck to get a better look at their charge. No doubt he'd be down at the security office the first chance he got. He'd have questions. They all would.

They kept moving toward the administration building. The security office had a reinforced panic room, much smaller than the one under the camp but useful for situations like this. They'd stick the trespasser in there while they figured out what to do.

The manuals they'd helped write said to turn the trespasser over to the local authority, the park rangers. But since she was a selkie, they'd be calling in the Tribunal. Enforcers would be here within hours to deal with her and evaluate the breach.

"Is there any point to interrogating you before the Enforcers get here?" Jackson asked, grunting as he and Jordan lifted her up the stairs. She'd gone limp the moment they'd cuffed her, so they'd been carrying her by her armpits.

She was silent. Jackson took that as a no. He helped Jordan get her secured to a chair in the panic room before stepping back outside to make the call. Anne Marie should be the one to report it, but the dispatcher would ask for a full report, and she wasn't trained to give scene updates.

"Jackson Berrings, Central District 172, calling in an intruder at Camp H.O.W.L.," he said when dispatch picked up. "Suspect is an adult female selkie, affiliation unknown."

"Copy that, Enforcer Berrings," a crisp voice answered. "We have East Coast Tribunal Enforcers on the ground in Kansas. Can you confirm Camp H.O.W.L. has an accessible helipad?"

They did. Campers weren't allowed to arrive or depart using the helipad because they would have to file a flight plan and the camp wanted to stay under the radar with the FAA. But the Tribunal operated with the clearance of a secret government agency and had no such restrictions.

"Affirmative," Jackson said. "Please update me with their arrival time, and I will meet them at the helipad."

"Dispatch will alert you when the team is twenty minutes out. Are you or any of the civilians in any immediate danger?"

"We are not. The suspect is in custody and secured. I have trained backup on-site. We will wait for further instructions from the Tribunal."

"Copy that. Stay safe, Enforcer Berrings."

The line went dead, and Jackson looked up to see Anne Marie and the man from the porch approaching. She looked livid.

"You will wait in my office until further notice," she told the man, who continued on while she stopped in front of Jackson.

"You have the intruder? Is it true she's a selkie?"

Jackson nodded. "We don't have a name or a motive yet, but we confiscated a camera bag and some high-end tools. My bet is she was hoping for a shot of Candice to sell. She may be a professional photographer. We're not sure how she knew Candice was here, though. That's our main concern at the moment." He waved his phone.

"I've already called it in. Enforcers will be here within the hour, I'd guess."

Anne Marie shot him a shrewd look. "*You're* an Enforcer. Do we really need to bring more in? That's just going to further traumatize my wolflings. Having men the size of tree trunks traipsing through camp in full tactical gear won't do much for their nerves."

Jackson looked down at the T-shirt and jeans he'd retrieved from the boathouse after he realized Jordan had the suspect detained. He could still smell the pink lemonade.

"I'm a district Enforcer," he reminded her. "I don't have clearance for this kind of issue. She'll go before the East Coast Tribunal. That's not something I can do."

She pursed her lips. "Why didn't she get farther?"

Jackson raised an eyebrow. "Excuse me?"

"She's a selkie. She shouldn't have been stopped by the fences."

"The second fence has barbed wire to deter humans, but it also has an alarm system that's triggered when an infrared beam is interrupted. It makes the siren here in camp sound like a lullaby. When Jordan got to her, she was on the ground writhing in pain. It's debilitating."

Anne Marie narrowed her eyes. "And I didn't know about this because…."

He shrugged and wished he could look away from her Alpha posturing. It was uncomfortable. "The Tribunal requires it for all camps built after 1997. We had a string of violence from the Were separatists in the late nineties, and all new construction had the supernatural alarm system installed. When Jordan and I were updating your systems, we added it."

"That doesn't tell me why I didn't know about it. That could have been a wolfling out there, Jackson! What if one of our campers set it off?"

"This is exactly why you didn't know about it," he said. "It's between the electrified fence and the outer perimeter fence. The likelihood of a wolfling triggering it is slim to none because the electric fence would stop them. We protect that with the inner fence that denotes the boundaries of camp, and I don't think you've ever had a wolfling cross that, have you?"

"No," she admitted.

"Every camp director in the country has the same reaction when they find out about the added defense. Luckily, they only find out if it is triggered. So welcome to the club. No, you cannot opt out of it. Yes, it was installed at the request of the Tribunal, since the security overhaul qualified as a major renovation. All camps built before the system was invented are required to add it when they update."

She sighed and pointed at him. "No more improvements to my camp without my knowledge."

He held his hands up. "I was just following orders. But I can promise you I don't have any plans to renovate anything else here at Camp H.O.W.L. or do anything to disrupt your routine."

She stared at him for a moment and rolled her eyes. "You smell like lemonade and sex. Go change. And tell Harris I need that report written up and on my desk in the next hour."

He didn't object. She could smell Harris on Jackson's clothes too, no doubt. Besides, finding Harris was at the top of his list.

Jackson shot off a quick text to Jordan updating him on the plans and then took off for the infirmary, the last place he'd seen Harris. Wolflings were milling around the pond, sitting together in clumps and all talking quietly.

Harris, Kenya, and Nick were on the porch, and Drew was taking around a tray of sodas and snacks for the kids.

"Anne Marie needs a report from you in an hour," he told Harris before swooping in for a soft kiss.

Harris's cheeks turned pink, but he looked pleased, his scent spiking with affection when Jackson wrapped an arm around his waist to keep him close. He knew Harris had never been in danger, but it was still reassuring to touch him and confirm he was all right.

"It's about Richard," Harris said. "I was just telling everyone about it. He was hiding in the bunker and refused to go patrol his section, and he actually called Candice out on this all being her fault. It was bullshit. Anne Marie is firing him right now. I have to write up the incident report so she has it for her files. I don't think he's going to go willingly, so you may need to help her."

That was part of his job as a district Enforcer. He wasn't called into service often, but when he was, it was to resolve minor spats or help cover up potential exposure incidents.

"I'm not her favorite person right now," he admitted. "But in an hour or two this place will be crawling with regional Enforcers. There won't be a shortage of people to help her toss him out."

"What can you tell us about the intruder?" Nick asked, swiping an iced tea from the tray Drew brought in.

"It was a selkie with a camera. I imagine she wanted to get photos for a tabloid. We won't interrogate her until the other Enforcers get here. This level of breach is their jurisdiction. Especially since she's a selkie."

"Why?" Drew asked. "What does her being a selkie have to do with it?"

"Selkies and most other shifters have a treaty with the Tribunal," Jackson explained. "They have representation on the Tribunal court and in exchange allow the Tribunal to act as their governing body. It's been like that for more than a century. Since she's a selkie, she's ours to deal with. If she'd been fae, we'd have handed her over to the fae court."

Nick shivered. "I've met one fae in my life, and that was enough."

They were intense. And they hated Weres since they thought Weres and shifters were the biggest threat to exposure for the supernatural community. Most supes didn't even try to blend with the outside world, while Weres and shifters had thrived for centuries by passing as human.

"I've got to get a shower and a change of clothes before the Enforcers arrive," Jackson said. "If you'll excuse me."

Jackson's stomach did a happy flip when Harris hurried out of the room after him.

"I don't think I have time for that kind of shower," Jackson said as they made their way upstairs.

Harris pounced as soon as they entered Jackson's room. He kissed Jackson like a man starved for affection, and Jackson kissed him back just as desperately. He wished he had more time so they could burn off this nervous energy. Added to the sexual tension, all the adrenaline had Jackson itching to do something physical.

"I really do have to shower," he murmured as he pulled away. He unbuttoned his shirt, his knees going weak when Harris batted his hands aside and did it for him, followed by the clasp on his jeans.

"Do you have any idea how sexy you are when you take charge?" Harris asked, his voice husky. His dark silky hair was mussed, and he looked like sex on a stick. "God, Jackson. I thought seeing you in uniform was bad, but to have you barking out orders and explaining Tribunal policies—I don't even know what to do with you."

The confession surprised a laugh out of Jackson. He wasn't sure how he should respond. "I'm sorry I'm so competent at my job?"

Harris hummed as he helped Jackson toe off his shoes and step out of his jeans. "I'll go run you a shower, and then I'm going to leave before I embarrass myself."

Jackson's hand shot out and grabbed Harris, stopping him. "You could never embarrass yourself in front of me," he said, a smirk curving his lips as he traced the outline of Harris's cock through his pants. "Especially by admitting how aroused I make you."

Harris's eyes fluttered shut, and he groaned as Jackson teased him through the fabric. "Maybe you'd better start your own shower," he rasped out.

Jackson grinned and leaned in to give him a hard kiss. "I will. You should go shower too. Think about what I'm doing in here while you're in yours."

Harris's eyes shot open, his pupils so dilated they looked black. "I'm going to make you pay for this."

"For what?" Jackson asked innocently. "Caring about your hygiene and general well-being?"

Harris flipped him off. "For making me walk back to my cabin with a raging hard-on," he muttered. "Asshole."

Jackson grinned. "I'll be more than up for playing with your hard-on later, assuming you don't exhaust yourself in the shower."

Harris grunted at him and walked out, leaving Jackson standing naked in the middle of the guest room. He glanced at his watch and cursed. It would have to be a fast shower if he was going to be ready in time to meet the Enforcers. Jackson looked down, palming himself with a sigh. Maybe he wouldn't hurry *too* much.

DISPATCH called a few minutes after Jackson had gotten dressed. He wished he had his tactical uniform, but all he had were borrowed sweats, because his jeans had honey and goat cheese smeared all over them.

It wasn't the best impression to make on the Enforcers he hoped would soon be his colleagues, but he'd have to make do.

Four of them exited the helicopter, jumping out when it was six feet off the ground instead of waiting to land. They moved with an almost eerie precision, and inexplicable pride warmed Jackson's chest as they ran across the field toward him. These were Weres who had trained their whole lives for this position, and he could be running beside them in less than a month.

The helicopter veered back up and disappeared. It had been less than two minutes from the moment he'd heard it on the horizon—that was beyond impressive.

"Enforcer Berrings?" one of the regional Enforcers shouted from a few feet away.

"Yes, ma'am," he said, standing at attention as they approached.

"Enforcer Abernathy. I'll be the lead on this case. Can you brief us while you're taking us to the suspect?"

Jackson gave them the rundown, wishing he had more to add. Jordan was with the selkie, and she still wasn't talking, so aside from giving them an inventory of the contents of her camera bags, he had no new information.

She hadn't been carrying any weapons aside from the wire cutters she'd used on the outer fence. The rest of the equipment had been cameras and telephoto lenses.

"You said the suspect is a selkie? Did she have her skin with her?"

"No. It's possible she was being coerced, but I think it's more likely she just keeps it somewhere safe."

Abernathy nodded. They jogged up the stairs, and Jordan met them at the top.

"This is Jordan Garrison of the Garrison Pack in St. Louis. He runs Fang and Fury, the security company that did Camp H.O.W.L.'s recent upgrade."

Abernathy shook Jordan's hand. "We can take things from here," she told him. "I'm told you secured the suspect. Thank you for your assistance."

Jordan looked like he wanted to protest, but Jackson shook his head. The Tribunal was notoriously secretive. Civilians weren't allowed to participate in Tribunal proceedings.

"We'll take it from here," Abernathy said with a curt nod. "Berrings, we will update you when we find out more."

The four Enforcers disappeared into the panic room, the door shutting behind them.

"Well," Jordan said, staring after them and looking flustered. "Hello to you too."

"They're just doing their job," Jackson said, trying to pretend he hadn't been stung by the dismissal as well.

Jordan snorted. "And you're sure you want to join that?"

He was. He might not like their methods, but they got results. They'd all been stone-faced and brutally efficient, which made it easy to see why they didn't allow any outside affiliations. When you were a high-level regional Enforcer, it wasn't just a job. It was everything. They relied on each other for protection in horrible situations—a nonviolent intruder at a camp was practically a vacation for them.

He understood why they couldn't have any ties, but it wouldn't make it any easier to walk away from Harris if he was called up. *When* he was called up, he corrected himself. His father always told him confidence was more than skin-deep. He needed to believe it.

"Let's go repair the fence," he told Jordan. He was itching to do something—anything—useful. Fixing the fence beat waiting around and twiddling his thumbs.

When they got out to the perimeter fence, they found the hole already fixed. Whoever did it hadn't just patched the hole, they'd replaced the entire section. Smart, because it meant there were no weak joints that would make it easier for an animal or another intruder to force their way in.

"Things run too smoothly around here," Jordan muttered, stuffing his borrowed work gloves back into the tool bag they'd found in the machine shed.

"It was probably George. He handles all the maintenance."

Jordan picked up a stick and threw it aimlessly. "I'd say we could go take over the security office, but the Enforcers are still there. Is there anything else we should be doing?"

"Maybe some research to see how she pegged Candice as a Were? Something circulating on blogs must have tipped her off. Unless she was just covering all the bases and got lucky."

He pulled out his phone and shot off a group text as they walked, asking for a loaner computer since the security building was off-limits. Harris's answer to the group pinged almost immediately, and Jackson couldn't help but grin as he opened it.

My laptop is in my cabin, you're welcome to it.

Before he could respond, Harris sent a follow-up to him alone.

That was an invitation to be waiting in my bed for me, by the way. And to use my laptop. Can't wait to finish what we started.

Jackson fumbled with the phone, eager to answer, only to drop it when white-hot pain seared across his forehead.

He jumped back, his ears buzzing. The blaze on his face settled to a stinging simmer, and a beat later his hearing returned in full force. The first thing he registered was Jordan's hysterical laughter.

Jackson's muscles ached. He raised a shaky hand up to his forehead. The skin was blistered and hot.

"You," Jordan wheezed out. Tears were streaming and he could barely stand upright. He propped his hands on his thighs. "You—the fence. And bzzzzt!"

Jackson followed Jordan's gaze over his shoulder. The electric fence. He'd walked right into it.

"…can't believe… texting lover boy and…."

Most of the words were unintelligible, garbled from Jordan's laughter and gasps for air.

Jackson dove into the leaves, looking for his phone. He'd been texting Harris, and he hadn't been paying attention. Hopefully he hadn't fried it. God, he was never going to live this down.

Chapter Nine

"**YOU** handled yourself very well today, Candice. It was a scary situation, and you did everything right."

Candice was curled into a chair, looking more like the timid kid Harris had met two weeks ago than the boisterous wolfling she'd blossomed into. Setbacks were to be expected, but it made his blood boil to think a staffer had been the one to trigger the regression. She'd spent her life trying to please others and moving from one acting job to another. She brought that same attitude into therapy, which made her a challenging patient. He'd had to set boundaries early on because she was more than willing to dive in on topics and was excellent at mirroring what he wanted to hear back at him. She'd learned it from a former agent, the person who had told her she was fat at age eight. Luckily Candice's parents had noticed and gotten her new representation, but the damage had been done. He wished they'd gotten her into therapy back then, but now was better than never.

She'd barely had any time to grow into herself, so busy living up to what directors and fans thought she should be she'd never had time to discover who she actually was. They were working on shoring up her self-confidence, but Candice's critics had been hammering it down for the last decade—it was going to take more than a few weeks to fix it. Not only had she been bullied and threatened, it had been by someone she trusted, in a safe space. Richard had done more than just shoehorn her back into that Hollywood starlet box—he'd taken away the fragile peace she'd found here. Harris could kill him.

"I know you heard what Richard and some of the other wolflings said, but those attacks had more to do with them than you. You can't control how others see you, and I'm sorry some people have such a distorted view of who you are. But you know it's not true. Just like you know what happened today wasn't your fault."

"But it was! She wouldn't have come here if it wasn't for me. And now more people are going to come, and it's all my fault. I've ruined everything."

Harris stood up and paced over to the windows. He'd met with all his wolflings to check in with them, saving Candice for last because he'd known she'd need the most time. It was dark out, and he tried not to think about Jackson out there somewhere waiting for him. He hoped he hadn't already left for Lexington.

"Candice, we are not responsible for the choices others make. This selkie already knew about Camp H.O.W.L. She's with the Tribunal now, and they will make sure she doesn't tell anyone where you are or why you are here."

The Enforcers left hours ago, taking the selkie with them. She'd admitted she wanted photos to sell to the tabloid magazines, but she'd sworn she wasn't going to reveal the location or name of Camp H.O.WL. There were a ton of rumors swirling around on paparazzi message boards, and right now all of them were focusing on the plane that brought Candice to Lexington. The flight plan had been leaked by someone a few days ago, so photographers descended on Lexington trying to figure out where she'd gone. The consensus among the media was rehab, but they hadn't been able to confirm she was a patient at any of the hospitals or rehab centers in Kentucky. It was just a matter of time before they widened the search and found Camp H.O.W.L. It was on the books as a medium-security boot camp for juvenile delinquents, so hopefully it wouldn't rise to the top of any of their lists.

They'd deal with that if it happened. For now, he needed to pull Candice back out of her shell and undo the damage Richard caused.

"We've talked about how you'll keep your secret while you're in the spotlight," he said, switching gears. "And you've got solid plans for that. But have you thought about if you *want* that? Is acting something that brings you joy?"

Candice looked up, brow furrowed. "I love acting. I can't imagine myself doing anything else."

Harris leaned on the edge of his desk. "I'm a little surprised to hear that, considering how much you've shared that you hate all the attention."

She deflated. "I don't like that side of the business. I just want to act and be left alone."

"That's not a realistic goal," he said gently. "You're already one of the most recognizable faces in Hollywood."

"I know," she said. "I'm buying an estate in Wyoming. A ranch. And that's where I'll live when I'm not filming. I want to adopt racehorses who can't compete anymore."

"That's a good goal. Why retired racehorses?"

"Because once they've served their purpose, people just throw them away. Like they don't have any value anymore once they can't run."

Now they were getting somewhere. "Are you afraid that at some point the same will happen to you in Hollywood?"

She smiled grimly. "I know it will. But when it does, I'll have a nest egg to fall back on, and I'll have my ranch. Maybe I'll open it up to Were families as a vacation spot. Somewhere they can be themselves without worrying about someone seeing."

"There are a few places like that. It's not a bad idea. I like that you're planning for the future and that you've identified something outside your career that makes you happy."

There was a retreat in upstate New York run by selkies that had lakeside cabins supernatural families could rent. It had a human compound too, a hotel with massive indoor waterslides and pools. The regular hotel served as a cover for the supernatural families who visited. It also subsidized the cost of the cabins by the lake to make them affordable for all supes.

"I wanted to go through the Turn like a normal person," she said, her tone resigned. "I should have known that wasn't possible."

"It is possible. You're just another wolfling here, Candice. I know we've had to make some changes to accommodate that, and not all of your fellow campers appreciate that, but no one begrudges you this experience. Trust me. In twenty years, all of you will look back at this and laugh. And I hope you'll remember it as a time you were able to be yourself and relax. Everyone needs that. It sounds like the ranch you're buying will be an excellent place to do it."

Her smile was stronger this time, and she nodded. "Can I head back to my cabin now? Kayla said she'd get stuff to make s'mores, and we're going to have a fire outside."

Now she sounded like any other nineteen-year-old wolfling. A weight lifted off Harris's chest.

"Of course. Have a good night."

Harris locked up his office as soon as she'd left and hurried over to the infirmary. Jackson was sitting on the front steps with a beer in his hand, watching Nick and Jordan play some ridiculous game with balls attached to strings and a ladder in the dark. It would seem strange anywhere else, but they didn't have to hide their supernatural abilities here at Camp H.O.W.L. Playing a game in the dark wasn't a problem for someone with preternatural night vision.

Jackson hopped up when he saw Harris, his eyes flashing.

"Everything okay with the kids?"

Harris nodded. "Everyone is coping well. We'll see what tomorrow brings, but they're doing okay tonight."

"And how are you doing, doctor?" Jackson asked, looping his arms around Harris's shoulders.

He could feel the beer bottle clunk against his back, but he ignored it in favor of leaning in to give Jackson a kiss. "Better now that I'm here," he said.

"We're all better now that you're here," Jordan called from the lawn. "He's been pining."

"So much pining," Nick agreed as he lined up his next shot.

Jackson flushed an adorable shade of pink but didn't deny it. Harris grinned and tugged on his waist, urging him away from the house. "Why don't we go back to my cabin?"

Jackson lobbed his beer bottle toward the recycle bin on the porch, wincing when it shattered as it hit another bottle inside. Drew yelled something expletive-laden from inside the house.

"Don't worry, I'm taking him off your hands," Harris yelled back.

Jackson huffed out a laugh and let Harris lead him down the walkway. "I wish our first night together could have been under better circumstances."

Anticipation shivered up Harris's spine. Jackson said *first*. That implied he saw them having more than one night together. That was good news. Harris wanted all the nights he could get.

"I'm sorry my sessions ran so late and wrecked our plans."

"Circumstances," Jackson said with a shrug. "Your job comes first. So does mine."

The edge in his voice was clear. It was a reminder there was an expiration date on whatever was going on between them.

Harris forced himself to smile. He wasn't going to waste any of their precious time together. He could mope later.

"For tonight, I'm hoping *you* come first," he teased. "I have plans for you. Are you still heading back to Lexington?"

"No. Anne Marie wants us on-site for a meeting tomorrow, and the Tribunal has recommended at least one of us stays until Candice is off the property. You're stuck with me. I've already cleared it with the department. My CO knows something's up. I think he's realized I'm on my way out."

Harris wished he could be happy without reservation at the news that Jackson was staying. He should be—he'd made the decision to live in the now, hadn't he? That meant not borrowing trouble, as Nick liked to say. He hated that his joy at having his mate all to himself was tempered with sadness.

He nearly stumbled when Jackson grabbed him by the belt loops and yanked him back as he was climbing the stairs to his cabin. Jackson saved him from falling by pressing up against his back, caging him in a warm embrace.

Harris turned his head and looked back at Jackson, laughing. "Wha—"

Jackson leaned forward and kissed him. Harris's neck twinged at the awkward angle, but he didn't care. This playful, flirty side of Jackson wasn't something he'd seen before, and he loved it.

He groaned when Jackson tightened his arms around him, stopping Harris from turning to sink into the kiss. A thrill ran up his spine when he realized how much stronger Jackson was. As a Were, Harris was used to being stronger than his partners—or at least on equal footing when he slept with another werewolf. There was no question Jackson was stronger, though. Harris's pulse throbbed at the knowledge he couldn't move if Jackson didn't want him to. He'd had no idea that was a kink of his until now. Though it was more that it was *Jackson* doing the restraining. He had a kink for anything involving his mate.

"No, no, no," Jackson muttered against his lips. "What are you doing? You're going the wrong way.

I want my mouth on your dick like, *yesterday*. No moving backward. Get inside."

Harris wanted to protest he had been heading inside when Jackson ambushed him with a kiss, but he'd lost the ability to speak when Jackson mentioned his mouth. He went weak in the knees when Jackson dove back in for another kiss, this time sliding a hand down to cup over Harris's erection. Harris leaned all his weight against Jackson, pressing his ass against Jackson's crotch.

"Inside," Jackson growled.

Jackson's cock was rock hard and felt perfect pressing against Harris's ass. Harris whined when Jackson broke the kiss and pushed him forward, his legs like Jell-O as Jackson guided him up the rest of the stairs onto the porch.

Harris managed to open the door, and the moment it closed behind them, Jackson spun Harris around, pinning him to it.

"The sounds you make are going to fucking kill me." Jackson pressed his thigh against him, and Harris rutted against it, groaning at the way the solid heat of Jackson's muscular thigh provided just enough friction to send pleasure sparking through him.

"You have no idea how long I've been waiting for this," Harris blurted. He'd regret being so open later, but right now he was drunk on his mate's pheromones.

Jackson leaned in and mouthed against his neck, and Harris tilted his head to the side to give him more room. His nerve endings were on fire. When Jackson licked a stripe from his jaw to his ear, Harris bucked his hips, desperate for more contact.

His reward was a light nip against the thin skin of his jaw, which made his wolf practically stand up and sing. It wasn't a mating bite, but the mere sensation of Jackson's teeth against his skin was the sexiest thing Harris had experienced in his life. He wrapped trembling arms around Jackson's broad shoulders and held him there, his own breaths coming in gasps nearly drowned out by the pounding of his heart.

"I can't think about anything but you," Jackson muttered as he kissed his way up Harris's jaw. He rested their foreheads together, and Harris realized Jackson was breathing just as hard as he was.

"What you smell like," Jackson continued, burying his face in Harris's wild hair and taking a deep breath. "What you taste like." He dipped back down for a quick kiss that was almost chaste compared to what they'd been doing. "And now that I know what you sound like—" He pressed his thigh against Harris's erection and elicited a groan from deep in Harris's chest, "The noises you make are going to haunt my dreams. Fuck, Harry."

Harris's fangs itched, threatening to burst through his gums. He wanted to bite Jackson. To mark him as his mate. To stake his claim so everyone who saw Jackson knew he belonged to someone.

But he couldn't. Jackson didn't want it, and even though it was physically painful, Harris was going respect his mate's wishes. There was one thing he didn't have to hold back on, though. He wanted Jackson writhing and naked, and he was allowed to have it.

Harris tugged at Jackson's T-shirt, pulling it up over his head when Jackson backed off enough to let him. He'd changed back into his jeans at some point, which was a shame. Jackson's ass looked amazing in Harris's sweats. Harris fumbled with the button, desperation making his fingers clumsy. He whined when Jackson batted his hands away, but he stopped resisting when he saw that Jackson was unfastening his jeans himself. He shucked them with an easy motion, letting them pool at his feet.

Harris dropped to his knees and mouthed at Jackson's precome-damp boxers. Those were Harris's, too, and the sight of Jackson's thick thighs straining the cotton was enough to make Harris's cock jump in his pants. He snaked his tongue through the slit in the fabric, his eyes fluttering shut when Jackson's bitter-musky flavor exploded across his tongue. Jackson groaned loudly, and Harris opened his eyes in time to see Jackson reaching out to brace himself against the door. His legs were shaking, and pride burst through Harris at the realization he'd been the one to reduce his strong mate to such weakness.

Harris slid his fingers into the waistband of Jackson's boxers and wiggled them down a few inches, exposing smooth skin. He ran his tongue over the ridge of muscle at his hip, enjoying the way gooseflesh spread along Jackson's skin as he delved deeper. He pressed light kisses along Jackson's treasure trail, pressing his nose to the skin and reveling in the scent of his mate's arousal.

He nuzzled into Jackson's thigh, the hair tickling against his cheek. Jackson rested a hand on his head, his fingers kneading Harris's scalp. Harris's wolf would have purred if it could.

Jackson tightened his grip in Harris's hair when Harris nosed against his cotton-covered erection. Harris tilted his head up and looked at Jackson, who was staring down at him with lust-blown pupils.

"You're still dressed." Jackson's voice was huskier than Harris had ever heard it.

Harris scrambled to stand up, nearly tripping in his haste to get his clothes off. His shirt joined Jackson's on the floor, and he toed off his shoes as he struggled with his belt. Jackson had gotten rid of his shoes, and Harris's eyes were glued to him as he shucked his boxers.

Harris had imagined this moment countless times, but the reality was so much better than the fantasy. His gaze slid past Jackson into the darkened main room of the cabin. His bedroom was down the hall, but he didn't think they'd make it that far. Hell, the couch was three feet away, and even that was a stretch.

Jackson took the decision out of his hands when he crowded Harris back against the door. The wood was cold on his back, and it felt good to his overheated skin. Jackson's mouth was on his again, and Harris lost himself in the kiss. His blood was pounding through his veins, and every breath he took was full of Jackson's scent.

Harris ran his hands up Jackson's back, mapping out all the dips and curves of his muscles. He found a ticklish spot along his rib cage and filed the information away for later, intent on mapping every inch of Jackson's body.

They both flinched when Jackson's phone rang. His jeans were pooled on the floor by their feet, and Jackson kicked them away. The ringing didn't stop, but a moment later Harris's phone started to ring as well.

"Fuck me," Jackson breathed out through gritted teeth.

"I've been trying," Harris muttered as he crouched down to grab his phone out of his pants. "It's the security office."

Jackson's phone had finally stopped, but Harris answered his and put it on speaker. Jordan's exasperated sigh filled the room.

"Would you tell your boyfriend it's a violation of his contract with Fang and Fury not to pick up his goddamn phone when it rings?"

"You can tell my boss to shove it," Jackson said.

"Your boss has heard your concern and tells you to go fuck yourself," Jordan answered. "We might have a problem. Two different patrols reported feeling like they're being watched when they're out in the woods. It could be paranoia, or it could be surveillance."

Harris tried to pull his shirt back on, but Jackson took it out of his hands and tossed it into the living room. He ran a hand over Harris's bare ass, making Harris shiver.

"And you need to tell me this right now because…?"

"Because I'm stuck in the control room, and I need someone I trust out there. These people don't have the training to ferret out a surveillance team."

Jackson groaned. "Give me twenty."

"Ten."

"Don't push it," Jackson growled. He disconnected the call and leaned around Harris to put his phone on the table near the door.

"I wanted to take my time with you, but it looks like that's going to have to wait." He kissed Harris, hard and wet, and wrapped a hand around both of their cocks. "Was gonna take you apart piece by piece, Harry. Have you begging for my dick by the end."

Harris was glad Jackson still had a hand on his ass because he might have collapsed without the support. Jackson's strokes were fast and too dry, but Harris had been on edge since their picnic. It wasn't going to take much to get him there.

He leaned into Jackson, resting his head against the crook of his neck. A few strokes in and his toes were already curling. He wrapped a hand around Jackson's bicep, feeling the way his muscles tightened as he worked them over. Harris gave in to instinct and licked at the sweat-damp skin of Jackson's neck, and that was all it took to send both of them spiraling over the edge.

Harris's entire body clenched as he came, his senses so overwhelmed that he had to shut his eyes. Their scents were mingled to such an extent it was difficult to tell where one of them ended and the other began. Sweat, arousal, come—all of it blended together until Harris couldn't smell Jackson; all he could smell was *them*.

As soon as the tremors of his orgasm eased, Jackson let him go. He pressed a kiss to Harris's nose. "I've got to get out and patrol. When I get back, we'll go for round two, yeah?"

Jackson ducked into the bathroom off the kitchen, and Harris looked at their clothes scattered around the room. They hadn't done anything more than make out and share a hand job, and Harris was more sated than he'd ever been in his life. He couldn't even begin to imagine what they could do if they had the luxury of time.

"Why don't I go out with you?" Harris asked when Jackson reappeared with a damp washcloth. He'd already wiped himself down, which made Harris's wolf want to whine at the loss of their scent. Instead, he took the cloth Jackson offered him and followed suit. It was bad manners to walk around smelling like a brothel. Washing wouldn't mask the scent entirely, but it would make it more bearable.

"While I would love to have you with me," Jackson said, leaning in for a quick kiss, "that doesn't sound very conducive to me actually getting any patrolling done."

Harris looked away when Jackson got dressed, focusing on getting his own clothes on. Getting undressed together had felt natural, but watching Jackson tie his shoes seemed too domestic.

"Why don't I go relieve Jordan in the control room? Then you both can patrol and cover twice as much ground."

With the added benefit of getting him back into Harris's bed sooner.

"That's a good idea."

Jackson checked his phone, wincing at a text message. Harris followed him out onto the porch.

"I'll go let Jordan know," Harris said. "Text me to let me know you're staying safe?"

Jackson hesitated, and for a moment Harris thought he'd gone too far. That was something a mate would ask, not a flavor-of-the-moment.

But Jackson nodded. "Sure. Let me know when you get to the control room, okay?"

Harris let out a breath he hadn't realized he'd been holding. "Sure."

Jackson took off in the direction of a path that led into the forest, and Harris made his way toward the center of camp. He hadn't made it more than a few dozen feet before he heard the alarms going off. Shit. This wasn't just paranoia.

Harris was probably the closest to the gates, so he decided to head there to secure them. He shot off a text to the group chat they used when they were out on patrol, seeing everyone checking in as their texts poured in. It was late, and all the wolflings were accounted for and going to the bunker, so he was fine to proceed to the gates.

During a lockdown, someone needed to run the perimeter outside the gates, so Harris let himself out through the walk-through panel. It locked behind him, and he started down the gravel to confirm the road was clear.

He heard heartbeats as soon as he broke through the trees. Headlights flicked on, illuminating the gravel drive and blinding him. Harris blinked and looked away, pain searing through his head as his eyes fought to adjust to the sudden wash of light.

"Put your hands up and identify yourself!"

"This is private property," Harris snapped.

"I'm Agent Cahoon with the FBI. Hands up and identify yourself."

Goddammit. This was the last thing they fucking needed right now.

Harris started to reach for his phone to call Anne Marie and Jordan, but stopped when his vision adjusted enough to see three people in front of him with weapons drawn.

"I'm going to get out my phone so I can call the director of this facility," Harris said, raising his hands. Getting shot might not kill him, but he'd still rather not. Besides, with three trained agents shooting, he very well could end up with a fatal headshot.

"Keep your hands where we can see them," Agent Cahoon barked. "We have a search warrant for the premises. Identify yourself and open the gates."

Like hell. They didn't exactly have protocol for the FBI coming with a warrant, so he'd go with the next closest thing—the procedure for dealing with park rangers and local law enforcement. Stall.

"My name is Dr. Harris Wick," he said, keeping his hands up. "Camp H.O.W.L. is an accredited psychological detention center for violent juveniles. I'm afraid I cannot let you in without my director and our facility's lawyers present. If you let me—"

"We are authorized to cut open these gates, Dr. Wick," Agent Cahoon said. "I suggest you save us the trouble and open them."

Harris could run faster than they could shoot, but that would cause more trouble in the long run. A human couldn't sprint that fast. Harris took a deep breath. He had to buy time for all the wolflings to get to the bunker. Jordan would be monitoring the situation from the cameras.

"I need to call the director."

"I'm getting tired of this game, Dr. Wick. Open the gate."

"It's not a game," Harris said, his arms going back up when an agent crept closer, gun still drawn. "You will not gain access to the facility without our director and our lawyers. If you'd like me to call her now, I'm happy to."

Two of the agents surged forward and knocked Harris to the ground. Knees pinned him to the gravel while someone cuffed him.

"Huntington, call for backup. We're going to have to cut the fence."

"Sir, we've tried," someone said. "It's not budging."

Harris couldn't bite back the grin at the string of curses that flowed out of Cahoon's mouth.

"Arrest him for obstruction. Owens, take him to the temporary field office we set up at the sheriff's department. I want to have him questioned. Somebody get me in touch with the facility director."

"There's a call button right there," Harris called out when two men picked up him up, holding him by his arms, and stuffed him into the back seat of an SUV.

Chapter Ten

"WHAT do you mean, the FBI took him?"

Even the unflappable Scott looked shaken. Jackson found him manning the security office when he'd raced back after hearing the FBI was at the gates.

"The agent arrested him when Harris refused to let them in," Scott said.

"How did they get to him? Why wasn't he inside the gates?"

Scott looked around, uneasy. Jackson took a deep breath to calm himself. He smelled like panic and desperation, which would put any Were on edge. He didn't need to add to this clusterfuck by making the people around him uncomfortable.

"The new protocol during a lockdown is for someone to run the perimeter and make sure the road is secure. He was the closest to the gates when the alarms went off." Scott looked up, hesitant. "It was one of the new policies Fang and Fury put in place."

Dammit. Jackson's skin prickled with the need to shift. Someone had taken his mate. His mate was in danger and worse, it was his fault.

"Jordan and Anne Marie are down at the gates now. She's got our legal team on the phone and someone will be here soon. I'm sure as soon as they get here we'll be able to figure out where they took Harris and get him back."

"Where they took him?" Jackson's voice cracked. Panic thundered through his chest. How could he plan to get his mate back when no one knew where he was? "We don't even know where he is right now?"

Scott put his hands out to placate him, stepping back when Jackson snarled at him.

Jackson blew out a breath and closed his eyes. He leaned against the wall, letting it ground him as he focused on getting his wolf under control. He was in situations like this all the time. Hell, most of the time he was the officer taking someone's loved one away. He could handle this. The FBI wasn't going to hurt Harris. Irritate him, sure. But they wouldn't injure him.

"Sorry," Jackson said once he was sure he was in control. "What do we know?"

"The FBI agents at the gate have a search warrant. Anne Marie says it looks legit. Our lawyers have calls in to Senator Edwards. They think he'll be able to get the judge to throw out the search warrant. After that I'm sure it will be easy to bail Harris out."

Jackson blew a breath out and nodded. "Do we know what tipped the FBI off?"

"The warrant says something about a report."

"The wolflings are in the bunker?"

"Safe and sound."

Jackson nodded. He pulled up a chair and took one of the open terminals to see if he could find anything about Camp H.O.W.L. circulating online.

"What does the warrant say? What are the grounds for the search?" he asked after another twenty minutes of fruitless digging.

"Anne Marie said they were looking for evidence of human trafficking. Kidnapping, that kind of stuff."

That was weak. It was an exploratory mission at best, since there was no evidence of any kind of wrongdoing. They'd be able to find a judge to toss it out. Who could have reported them for human trafficking? The selkie's family, maybe?

A car turned onto the drive, and Jackson zoomed the camera. He recognized the driver—it was one of the camp's legal team. Thank God. He and Jordan had used the same firm when they'd incorporated Fang and Fury.

The scene at the gate exploded into motion when the car drove up, but the lawyer didn't seem the slightest bit ruffled by the guns drawn on him. He got out of the car with his hands up, but moments later they let him pull out his identification and everyone stood down.

He also handed over papers that made the agent in charge furious, so it was probably an order rescinding the search warrant. The Good Old Boys network was alive and well, except most of these boys could sprout fangs or fur. Senator Edwards had highly placed friends, and not just werewolves. Those who weren't had other secrets they'd move heaven and earth to keep quiet.

"Jordan says Harris was taken to the Marengo Sheriff's station," Scott said, his fingers flying over the keyboard as he texted back.

Jackson got up, but Scott stopped him. "Another lawyer is already there. He says you don't—"

"Oh, I do," Jackson said, shaking his head. "Jordan knows better."

Scott smiled for the first time since Jackson walked in. "He says to tell you his keys are in the cup holder, and to give them ten minutes to disperse the FBI vehicles before you tear out of here."

HARRIS was waiting for him on the steps of the sheriff's office when he pulled up. He looked rumpled but not hurt. It likely had more to do with the sleepless night than his treatment.

"I'd have stopped to pick up a coffee for you, but this godforsaken place doesn't have a Starbucks," he said when Harris opened the door and slid into the passenger seat.

Jackson leaned across and kissed him before pulling away from the curb. The less time they spent here the better. He wanted to get Harris back to Camp H.O.W.L. so he could shower off all the foreign scents that were making Jackson's skin crawl.

"Not a lot of options out this way," Harris said, settling back into the seat. "That really sucked."

Jackson reached out and took his hand, squeezing it. Harris clung to him, so he didn't try to take it back. "I bet it did. You did good, though. I wish it hadn't been you out there, but you did everything right."

Harris closed his eyes and chuckled wearily. "And see where it got me."

Jackson wanted to pull the car over and do whatever it took to erase the worry lines from his mate's face. He settled for squeezing his hand again.

"I'm starving."

That, Jackson could do something about. He'd passed a twenty-four-hour diner on the highway. Four in the morning wasn't too early for breakfast, was it?

"Do you think you're up for a stop? We can grab something to eat on the way back."

Harris opened one eye. "Thelma's?"

"If that's the greasy spoon on 64, then yes."

Harris groaned. "They have the best blueberry pancakes."

The tightness that had taken over Jackson's chest hours ago eased. Harris was fine. Alive and unharmed and craving blueberry pancakes.

"It's a date."

Harris grinned and rubbed his free hand over his face. "I'd always envisioned myself a little more put together for our first date."

Hearing that Harris had imagined dating him thrilled Jackson more than he cared to admit. "I think our first date was lunch in the boathouse."

"God. Was that really yesterday?"

It was hard to believe. Once Jackson let himself admit his connection to Harris, things had snowballed. It felt like they'd been together for years, not hours. He already struggled to separate their history as friends from their brief time as lovers.

"It was, and it totally counts. You wooed me with food. Don't deny it."

Harris laughed. "Technically, Frank wooed you. I just asked him to make me a lunch to go."

Jackson pulled his hand back and clutched it to his chest in mock horror as he turned into the diner parking lot. "Did you catfish me with food?"

Harris's giggles were a little on the hysterical side, and as soon as he'd parked, Jackson rubbed his back. "C'mon, let's get some food in you."

"I'd rather have something else in me," Harris choked out between laughs.

God, so would Jackson. But right now, Harris needed food and sleep. They could indulge in the rest later. "Show me why these pancakes are the best," he said as he got out of the car. "I'm always an eggs and hash browns kind of guy at diners."

He held his arm out for Harris to take and closed the passenger-side door. Harris was capable of walking on his own, giggles aside, but Jackson liked the excuse to keep him close.

The diner was empty except for a waitress sitting behind the register with a magazine. Jackson grimaced when he recognized Candice's face splashed across it.

"Sit anywhere," the waitress said, not even looking up.

"Let's get a table. I have a feeling you'd slide right out of a booth, as out of it as you are," Jackson told Harris.

The waitress looked up, her eyes widening and her scent blooming with lust and surprise when she saw them. He almost laughed. Jackson doubted they were her usual early-morning fare.

She gave the hand he had curled around Harris a speculative look. "Your buddy have a few too many?"

Jackson bared his teeth in a possessive smile. "My boyfriend has been up all night, and he's a little loopy. If we could get some orange juice and a hot tea for him that would be great."

She looked doubly intrigued by that development, and Jackson wished he'd kept his mouth closed. Now she'd hover around them even more. But at least she wouldn't hit on Harris. He wasn't sure how his wolf would deal with that, and they'd had enough drama already today.

"Sure," she said after another lingering look. "My name's Michelle. I'll have that right out."

"She wants you," Harris whispered as Jackson settled him into a chair.

Maybe Jackson should have taken Harris home to sleep. Jackson could run two days with no sleep if he needed to, but he'd been trained to do it. Poor Harris clearly wasn't used to being so tired—he was almost drunk with exhaustion.

"She wants *you*, and I don't blame her," he teased, his pulse jumping at the way a sleepy smile curved Harris's lips. "I want you too."

"You have me," Harris said.

He didn't, though. Not to keep. He was going to walk away from this if the Tribunal wanted him. Every hour they spent together made Jackson a little less sure he could.

Michelle appeared with laminated menus for them, a carafe of orange juice, and Harris's tea, so Jackson buried that thought and busied himself with pouring Harris some juice.

"Have this first," he told him, eyeing him when Harris reached for the little jug of hot water instead. Weres had higher metabolisms than humans and needed to eat more to keep their blood sugar up, and Harris probably hadn't eaten anything since their interrupted lunch.

Harris rolled his eyes but downed the glass of orange juice while Jackson poured the steaming water into a mug and opened the tea bag for him. It was all so domestic, and Jackson wanted to hate it, but his wolf was luxuriating in it.

"What happened with the FBI? No one would tell me anything. The lawyer who came to spring me said everything was under control but didn't give me any details."

Jackson nudged a menu toward Harris and studied his own. "Anne Marie and Jordan held them off until the lawyers arrived, and Senator Edwards had the search warrant voided not long after that. No one got in."

"How long did the wolflings spend in lockdown?"

Of course he'd be more concerned about that than his own arrest and detention.

"About three hours. Not bad, considering the circumstances."

When they found out this time it was the FBI and not an intruder, they got angry instead of upset, which Nick said was a good thing. Jackson didn't see how a room full of angry wolflings was better than a room full of scared ones, but that was why Nick was the psychologist and Jackson was the muscle.

Harris nodded. "We'll probably have to add some sessions tomorrow. Or I guess it would be today, wouldn't it? Just to make sure they're processing."

Jackson reached out and put a hand on Harris's knee under the table. "How are *you* processing?"

Harris snorted out a laugh, then covered his mouth. "I'm sorry. It's just weird, hearing therapy speak from you of all people. I'm fine. Tired, annoyed, but fine."

That stung. Did Harris think he didn't care about him? "It's a legitimate question," he said defensively.

Harris covered Jackson's hand with his and squeezed his fingers. "It is. But you've got to admit, you've never been a talk-to-me-about-your-feelings kind of guy, Jackson."

Because he'd never had a mate before. Jackson barely stopped himself from snapping out the retort. He didn't want to complicate things further. It would be hard enough to walk away from Harris without admitting this was more than a fling.

"I didn't mean to hurt your feelings," Harris said, all traces of amusement gone. "I guess maybe I'm not dealing with it as well as I thought. Humor is a coping mechanism for me. It wasn't terrible. They threw me in a room and asked me a bunch of questions I refused to answer. They didn't have a chance to do much else before the camp's lawyer showed up."

Michelle popped over to take their orders before Jackson could pick at that statement. He knew how intense an interview room was, and he doubted the FBI agents had been happy when Harris refused to speak.

Harris ordered blueberry pancakes, and Jackson flicked a glance over the menu with a frown. It wasn't enough food for someone who hadn't eaten in more than sixteen hours.

"He'll have three eggs over easy too. And an order of turkey sausage, if you have it."

"Already at the ordering for each other stage of your relationship?" She grinned at Harris and winked. "Honey, this one's a keeper."

Jackson ignored the way his cheeks burned and ordered himself a breakfast platter with extra meat. He'd toss a few pieces of sausage onto Harris's plate when he wasn't looking.

They sat in comfortable silence until the food came, and aside from occasionally reminding Harris he needed to eat more, they were quiet through that too. It was one of the things he'd always loved about being with Harris. No awkward silences. They were both just happy to be in each other's presence. Looking back, it was kind of an odd thing to love about a friend. Maybe he'd known Harris was his mate all along, but his brain hadn't been ready to process it.

He wished it had waited a few more years.

When the pauses between Harris's bites stretched longer and longer, Jackson decided he was ready to go home. By the time he'd paid the check, Harris's head was pillowed in his arms on the table. Jackson was tempted to snap a photo because he looked adorable, but he resisted. If he ended up in New York, it would be one more string attaching them.

He hauled Harris up and walked him out to the car. "You can sleep on the way back," he told him when Harris grumbled.

Jackson buckled Harris's seat belt and closed the door quietly, leaning against it for a long moment. Was being an Enforcer worth giving this up? Harris had literally fallen asleep at the table, and it had still been the best date Jackson had ever had.

Harris slept through the rest of the drive, barely twitching when Jackson had a conversation with the staffer manning the gate. Jackson parked in the garage and wondered if he should put the seat down and leave Harris in the car.

The thought of Harris waking up confused and alone in the garage made his wolf whine, so Jackson resolved to carry Harris back to his cabin. It was just after five, so they weren't likely to run into anyone. He couldn't even imagine how much teasing they'd both have to endure if Scott or Kayla caught him carrying Harris across the camp bridal style.

Harris had curled in on himself as he slept, so it was a struggle to untangle him from the seat belt. He lifted him carefully, grinning like an idiot when Harris instinctively nestled into him. He tightened his grip under Harris's knees and nudged the car door shut. Thankfully all the doorknobs at Camp H.O.W.L. were optimized for shifted wolves, so he had no trouble getting out of the garage with his burden.

Jackson took a deep breath when they were outside, letting the scent of pine and dew fill his senses. He'd miss this when he was in the city.

Harris was still fast asleep when Jackson let himself into the cabin. The lingering scent of their come filled the entryway, making him shiver. Harris twitched in his arms.

Jackson hadn't been inside Harris's bedroom before, but he had no trouble finding it. Harris's scent was concentrated there, heady and warm. The bed hadn't been made this morning, so Jackson put Harris down in the nest of blankets and started undressing him.

Once he had him down to his boxers he pulled the mound of blankets over him, marveling at how many Harris kept on the bed. None of them smelled like stale detergent, which meant Harris actually used them all. Jackson ran hot when he slept and rarely used more than one on his bed.

He pulled a spare blanket off the easy chair in the corner and retreated to the living room. It was tempting to climb into bed with Harris, but they hadn't talked about sleeping together. He didn't know if Harris just wanted sex or if he wanted intimacy as well, and Jackson wasn't going to make that decision for him.

The couch wasn't the most comfortable one he'd ever slept on, but it would do. Especially since it smelled like Harris. Jackson drifted off almost as soon as his head hit the couch cushion.

He wasn't sure if it had been minutes or hours, but Jackson woke with a start when he felt someone run their fingers through his hair. He blinked open his eyes, and it took him a moment to focus on Harris's face hovering above his. It was dim in the living room, which meant it must still be before dawn.

"Need something?"

Harris looked at him a long moment before murmuring in a sleep-rasped voice, "You."

All vestiges of sleepiness fled when Harris lowered himself onto the couch, crowding against Jackson. Harris kissed him, tentative and soft, and Jackson wrapped his arms around him and rolled so Harris was resting on top of him.

"Thank Christ. When I woke up without you, I was afraid it meant you didn't want this."

Jackson thrust up against him, and Harris inhaled sharply.

"I get it. You want this."

"I do," Jackson said, pressing a light kiss against Harris's jaw. "I didn't know if you would want me in bed with you, so I came out here."

"I pretty much always want you with me, no matter where I am," Harris muttered, his breath hot against Jackson's cheek. "Would you come back to bed with me if I asked?"

Jackson leaned back so he could make eye contact. "Of course."

Harris's grin was electric. He started to scramble off Jackson, but Jackson locked his arms around him and held him in place.

"I carried you here. Did you realize that?"

Harris's cheeks flushed. "From the car?"

"All the way from the garage, yes. And the whole way I was thinking about how hot it was, having you in my arms. Knowing you trusted me enough to let your guard down like that." He loosened his hold on Harris. "Is it too weird to ask you if I can carry you to the bedroom?"

Harris's breath quickened. "It's not too weird."

Jackson sat up, careful not to dump Harris on the floor, and manhandled him into a position he could manage. The smell of Harris's arousal spiked, which Jackson found interesting. Though as much as he enjoyed moving Harris around like this, maybe it shouldn't be a surprise Harris liked it as much as he did. This was his mate, after all. They were supposed to be compatible in all things.

"Someday I want to hold you up against the door and fuck you," Jackson murmured as he stood. The burn in his muscles only added to his excitement. Harris was lean, but he wasn't light. There was a lot of strength coiled in those ropy muscles of his, but he was letting Jackson cradle him like something fragile and precious.

Harris groaned and buried his face against Jackson's neck. "Fuck."

"But right now, I want you on a bed. I want to take all the time we didn't get the first time around yesterday."

Harris palmed himself through his boxers and a wave of want crashed through Jackson hard enough to weaken his knees. He nearly tripped through the threshold to Harris's room. The bed was even messier than it had been when he'd come in earlier, and part of Jackson hoped it was because Harris had trouble sleeping without him.

He squashed that thought, since it would mean Harris would suffer when he left. He didn't want to think about that right now.

"Want to spread you out and worship every inch of you," Jackson murmured. He tossed Harris on the unmade bed and pounced on top of him, pinning him to the mattress.

He wanted to cover Harris with his scent, grind it into him until he reeked with it. Jackson's wolf wouldn't be happy until Harris bled Jackson's scent out of his pores. He wanted to mark and take.

He ran his tongue over the spot he ached to bite, the thick muscle at the juncture of Harris's neck and shoulder. Most Weres placed their mating marks on their partner's wrist these days, but Jackson wanted his to be something so much more intimate. Screw being civilized. He wanted his mark to be a clear brand, advertising his claim to everyone his mate met.

Not that Harris would be wearing his mark. But if he did bite him, it would be there.

Jackson nipped at the skin, and Harris cried out and bucked underneath him. His cock filled at his mate's unabashed arousal, throbbing when he realized he'd made faint impressions with his teeth. They healed in an instant, but they'd been there.

He canted his hips forward, desperate for friction. Harris gripped his back, his fingers digging into Jackson's skin and urging him closer. Jackson resisted, not willing for this to be over in a span of minutes. He pulled himself back, kissing away the frown on Harris's face as he protested the separation.

"I'm dying to get you naked," Jackson explained when Harris rose up on his elbows, trying to follow him to finish the kiss. "I can't get enough of looking at you. You're gorgeous."

Harris obligingly lifted his hips, letting Jackson peel his boxers down his thighs and toss them into the corner. Jackson sat back on his heels and drank in the sight in front of him. It was dark in the room, but he could still appreciate Harris's golden skin and the dips and valleys of his muscles. The hair around his cock was as dark as the hair on his head, but it wasn't the same silky texture. Jackson leaned forward and nuzzled his face into the unruly thatch and mouthed against Harris's balls, breathing in the heady scent of him.

Harris let out a guttural moan that went straight to Jackson's dick. Jackson shimmied out of his jeans and backed off enough to draw his shirt over his head. He slid up Harris's body, hissing out a pleasured gasp when they were finally skin to skin.

His flesh hummed like it was alight with a million tiny sparks. If it felt this good to be lying on top of Harris, what would it feel like to be *inside* him? Jackson shuddered at the thought, his already hard cock jumping against the jut of Harris's hip.

Jackson kissed him, and as soon as their lips met, it was like a circuit had been completed. The energy that buzzed along Jackson's skin surged, leaving him so aroused he was dizzy with it. Every part of him that touched Harris felt heated—like he was standing just this side of too close to a crackling fire.

Jackson reached out blindly, trying to open Harris's bedside table without interrupting the kiss. He groped over the cool wood, growling in frustration when he couldn't find the handle.

Harris's laugh vibrated against his lips. He sank his teeth teasingly into Jackson's bottom lip, and Jackson pulled away with a yelp.

Harris rolled as much as he could with Jackson on top of him and opened the drawer, triumphantly holding up a bottle of lube a second later. "This what you were after?"

Jackson grinned. "If you're such a smartass, why don't you prepare yourself?"

He'd expected Harris to laugh, so he was unprepared for Harris to rise to the challenge—literally. He slid back, sitting on his heels as Harris rose on all fours and presented himself to Jackson, ass in the air as he fingered himself open.

The sight stole the breath from Jackson's lungs. The roar of his pulse in his ears was so loud it almost drowned out the sounds of Harris's lubed fingers sliding in and out of his ass. Jackson whined, willing himself to calm down so he could commit the sight to memory.

His fingers twitched, aching with the need to touch. He balled them into fists and forced himself to sit back and watch. If he lunged forward now it would all be over far too soon. He ignored his throbbing dick, gaze glued to Harris's fingers as they eased their way in and out of his ass.

"I've never wanted anyone as much as I want you," Jackson confessed in a hushed whisper. It was both mortifying and freeing to admit it.

Harris moaned out a string of curses, his fingers sliding out. He rolled to his side, watching Jackson with heavily lidded eyes as he took care of his neglected erection with long, lazy strokes.

"How do you want me?"

Jackson's throat went dry. *Any way I can have you*, he thought.

"I want you to ride me," he said instead, his stomach flipping at the way Harris's eyes darkened. "I want to be able to see you."

He usually preferred not to face his partner when he had sex. That didn't feel right with Harris, and he liked that it would be something special he only shared with him, even if Harris didn't know that.

Jackson eased onto his back, and Harris was on him in a flash. He straddled Jackson and leaned forward to cup his hands on either side of Jackson's face. Harris held him like he was precious, and something inside Jackson shattered. He'd been holding back, but now he couldn't do anything but give all of himself to Harris. When Harris kissed him, it was tender and soft. Chest to chest, Jackson could feel Harris's heart pounding, just like his.

"I've waited years to have you like this," Harris whispered. He followed up the hushed words with another kiss, more insistent this time. Jackson wrapped his arms around Harris's back, letting his hands skate over the dips and planes of his muscles. The dimples at the base of Harris's spine were a perfect match for his fingers, and Jackson paused there to enjoy how well they fit together.

Harris sucked in a shaky breath and pulled back, sat up. He dug through the blankets for the lube and squirted a generous amount in his palm. Jackson nearly hit the ceiling when Harris wrapped his hand around his dick, giving it a teasing stroke as he coated it.

"No condom?"

Harris shook his head, his eyes reflecting the moonlight. "I don't want anything between us."

Jackson groaned. It wasn't uncommon for Weres to go without the condom if pregnancy wasn't a concern, but hearing Harris say it like that punched the air out of his lungs.

Jackson's hands steadied his hips as Harris rose and positioned Jackson's cock at his entrance. His eyes fluttered shut as he sank down, and Jackson swore his heart was in his throat as Harris lowered himself.

When he bottomed out, both of them let out a sigh. Jackson was afraid to move—he was already on the edge. Being face-to-face with Harris while he was buried inside him made him feel surprisingly vulnerable, and Jackson was glad Harris was the one in control.

Harris leaned in and kissed him again, like he sensed Jackson's mood. When he started moving, Jackson moved with him, trying his best not to break the kiss. He brought himself up on his elbows, chasing Harris's addictive taste as he delved into his mouth, his tongue mimicking the slow, steady strokes as Harris rolled his hips with agonizing slowness.

An electric tinge tweaked his gut at the same time Harris moaned. His fingers tightened around Jackson's biceps, and he drove down harder on his next stroke. Jackson broke the kiss and leaned his head back, letting it hang between his shoulders. Being inside Harris was overwhelming. Jackson had never been so in tune with a lover that he felt their pleasure along with his own, but he swore that was happening. His own release was building, his muscles clenching and burning. An unfamiliar pleasure coiled in his belly, spiking when Harris would groan or hiss out a breath.

Jackson let himself fall backward on the bed, freeing up his arms to reach for Harris. He caressed his hip with one hand and wrapped his other around Harris's cock, letting Harris fuck up into his fist on every upstroke. Harris threw his head back and closed his eyes, and the heat in Jackson's belly flared as Harris picked up the pace. Jackson wouldn't be able to hold out much longer, but it didn't seem like Harris would either.

As he tried to stave off his orgasm, Jackson's leg trembled. He wanted Harris to come first so he could feel him tighten around his cock. The mere thought had Jackson shuddering.

He switched up his strokes, curling his wrist so his palm teased across the head of Harris's cock. It only took a few more passes before Harris started to tense. The roller coaster of heat in Jackson's belly was a constant flame now, stoking his own arousal.

When Harris tightened around him and spurted come across their chests, he pulled Jackson over with him. Harris stilled, but Jackson bucked his hips up, chasing his orgasm as he sailed past the point of no return while watching his mate gasp out his name.

Harris dropped like a puppet whose strings had been cut, nuzzling into Jackson's chest. His ragged breath was loud in Jackson's ear, and an absurd sense of pride surged through Jackson.

He let Harris stay curled up on top of him for a few minutes until both of their breathing evened out.

"C'mon," he said, nudging Harris's hip. "We've got to get cleaned up."

Harris muttered but lifted himself up, grimacing when the movement dislodged Jackson's softening cock.

Jackson laughed and helped Harris roll to the side, peppering his face with kisses when it was in reach. Harris batted at him, irritated. He was already falling back to sleep.

Deciding to leave him be, Jackson got up and washed up in the bathroom, then brought back a warm washcloth to clean Harris up. He was out, barely protesting when Jackson swiped the cloth over him.

Jackson hesitated after he tossed the washcloth into the hamper. Should he get in bed with Harris? Was that too presumptuous?

Harris's hand shot out before he decided. He wrapped it around Jackson's wrist and tugged him onto the bed.

"Stop overthinking everything and come to bed," Harris murmured. "I want you here."

Jackson climbed under the covers and molded himself to Harris's back. He draped an arm across Harris's stomach, his heart skipping when Harris laid his own over it and twined their fingers together. Harris was already out, and Jackson listened to the steady beat of his heart as he drifted off himself.

JACKSON woke when the sun hit his eyes. Neither of them had thought to draw the blackout shades when they'd collapsed, and Jackson was too comfortable to get up and do it now. He was a master of sleeping when he needed to, since his shifts at the station were all over the place, but his mind was racing now. Waking up next to Harris made him feel complete in a way he hadn't known he was missing, and he was enjoying basking in it for the moment. Harris had burrowed into the blankets, visible only as tufts of unruly black hair. Jackson hadn't known he was a blanket hog. Or that he liked to curl up as he slept. Having that kind of intimate knowledge about Harris was oddly endearing.

His hip scraped against something cold when he tried to scoot closer to Harris's blanket burrito, and he dug under the sheets and pulled out his phone. It must have fallen out of his pocket when they'd climbed into bed. The battery was almost dead, but he saw a notification on the screen that stole his breath.

The Tribunal recruiter had emailed.

He opened it, eyes flying across the small screen and not believing what he was reading. He was in.

They wanted him. He was a regional Tribunal Enforcer. Part of the elite squad who carried out missions for the East Coast Tribunal, which governed everything from the Atlantic to the western borders of Louisiana up through Minnesota.

Elation swept through him. This was everything he desired. It would be a stepping stone to a position as a Second with any Pack he wanted. Retired Tribunal Enforcers could have their pick of Packs when they stepped down. In five, ten years, he'd be able to settle down and live out his dream as a Second in a strong Pack.

Harris mumbled something in his sleep, bringing Jackson's joy to a screeching halt. He couldn't ask Harris to wait that long for him. It wouldn't be fair to Harris, and it might even get Jackson killed. An unrequited mate bond was still a bond, and he'd be putting himself and everyone else on his team at risk if he joined the Enforcers with one intact.

Fuck.

Chapter Eleven

HARRIS knew something was wrong before he opened his eyes. He'd gone to sleep wrapped around Jackson, but now the only heartbeat in the room was his own.

Of course Jackson wouldn't stay. Why would he? They were just having fun, playing around with dating until he got called up to the big leagues. Harris was nothing more than a diversion to help him pass the time.

Which he'd known and agreed to. It didn't do any good to be bitter about it now. They were both adults, and he'd fully consented to being Jackson's good-enough-for-right-now.

He rolled over and buried his head in his pillow. It still carried Jackson's scent, which made him angrier at himself. He hadn't even been smart enough to do this in

Drew's guest room instead of bringing his mate's scent into his den. What had he been thinking?

The truth of it was, he hadn't been thinking. Not with his head anyway. Definitely not in the wee hours of the morning when he'd woken up exhausted, horny, and missing Jackson and heard him out on the couch. Or yesterday when they'd barely gotten across the threshold before Harris had rolled over and shown Jackson his proverbial belly.

Still, he should be able to enjoy the morning after before guilt and regret set in.

Harris rolled over and reached for his phone on the nightstand. It wasn't there, and he had a moment of panic before remembering he hadn't put himself to bed last night.

Jackson had folded his clothes from yesterday neatly on the chair. Harris reluctantly threw back the covers and forced himself to get up. He needed to go meet with Anne Marie and check in with Kenya and Nick about the game plan for counseling. They'd been through two stressful events in twenty-four hours; there was definitely going to be fallout. He wouldn't be surprised if a few fights broke out today because of the tension.

His phone was in the pocket of yesterday's jeans, but it was dead. He plugged it in next to his lamp and pulled on the jeans, the stale scent of the sheriff's holding cell mingling with Jackson's scent. He must have rubbed his palms on the fabric while he'd been folding it. Coincidence or attempt to mark him?

Either way, it didn't matter. Harris had been reading too much into things and overanalyzing everything Jackson did for the last two years. It was time to accept that sometimes an apple was just an apple, and a fuck was just a fuck.

Harris didn't want to waste time showering—*lie*; he didn't want to wash Jackson's scent off—so he washed his face and wet his hair, doing his best to tame it. He wandered back out into the bedroom as he brushed his teeth, tidying up. His boxers were in the middle of the floor, and the T-shirt Jackson had been wearing yesterday was puddled on the rug. Had he gone back to Drew's shirtless, or had he borrowed something clean?

Harris slipped the dirty shirt into a drawer by his bed. It would come in handy later when his wolf was howling for its mate after Jackson left.

He hesitated in the doorway and jogged back in, taking the shirt out and putting it in the laundry hamper. He was going to need a clean break when Jackson left. Keeping things that carried his scent would only draw out the process.

If Jackson was able to walk away, it meant Harris had no hope of ever completing a mating bond with him. Instead of nursing his unfinished bond, Harris was going to have to knuckle down and sever it. It was going to royally suck, but in the end it would be better to have a clean break than to let his wolf pine for Jackson.

IT hadn't been a coincidence that the FBI had come knocking. Harris's mind was still whirling at the news Anne Marie had delivered in their emergency staff meeting twenty minutes ago. Richard, the staffer who had been fired for refusing to follow protocol during the first breach, had gone straight to them.

Or rather, he'd gone straight to the nearest paparazzi he could find. He'd sold his story to them for $10,000, and the gossip rag that bought it called the FBI for comment. Richard hadn't exposed their secret,

but he'd painted a picture of Camp H.O.W.L. as a place
with disturbed teens and reckless staffers. One of the
stories he'd told them was how these teens—who were
all over the age of majority—were kept against their
will, committed by their parents.

That amounted to kidnapping, which made the
questions the FBI had thrown at him yesterday make a
lot more sense. There was also the question of how they
were able to operate on federal land, which was what
the main story of the day seemed to be. A few legitimate
news sources had picked up on that, and the gates were
crowded with photographers and reporters.

Luckily the clamor was removed from the
wolflings since only the administration building was
near the gates, but someone with a telephoto lens could
easily see farther into the camp.

Because of that, they were operating on a modified
lockdown. No wolflings were allowed outside unless they
were moving from building to building, and even then
they had to have a staff escort. Anne Marie unearthed an
old box of Camp H.O.W.L. baseball caps, and everyone
was wearing them with the brims pulled down.

Poor Anne Marie had been fielding calls from
concerned parents all morning. Harris didn't blame
them. The camp was in the spotlight, and the wolflings'
parents were right to worry about the staff's ability to
keep them safe.

Jackson and Jordan were stationed out by the gate,
stoic in reflective sunglasses and Camp H.O.W.L. polo
shirts. It was a blessing they hadn't packed their tactical
gear—Harris could only imagine the stories that would
crop up if it looked like they had military-style guards.

Unfortunately, all this craziness meant Harris
hadn't had a chance to talk to Jackson. As much as he

wanted to avoid him and nurse his ego, that wasn't the mature thing to do. He needed to have a face-to-face talk with Jackson so he could tell him this casual dating thing wasn't for him.

That wouldn't happen until after dinner at the earliest, thanks to Harris's full therapy load today, as well as the afternoon class he was teaching. It was even more important than ever now to make sure the wolflings were getting the best training they could provide. Today's seminar was about passing as human.

"You good? You look like you're a million miles away."

Harris offered Scott a weak smile. "Just trying to wrap my head around all this."

"Man," Scott said, shaking his head. "I heard the Tribunal has issued a warrant for Richard. He's in some deep shit."

The Tribunal was the least of his problems. There were a lot of angry Weres out there right now. Anne Marie could murder him with her bare, unshifted hands. Luckily for Richard, she was so busy handling this cluster she hardly had time to blink, let alone go hunting for him.

"I give no fucks about what happens to that dickbag," Harris said with a shrug. "But he's left us a giant mess here. I had three wolflings in my office before lunch crying and asking to go home. Anne Marie's phone is ringing nonstop between parents and the press, and she's making the senior staff take turns helping her answer it. I've been yelled at by more Alphas than I can count today, none of them mine."

Scott grimaced. "Yeah, that blows. I'm not sorry I wasn't tapped for it, though."

"It'll pass. We just need to ride it out."

That's what he'd been telling upset wolflings all day. He and Nick were planning to set up some fun activities later to help make up for the restrictive atmosphere. They'd do the scavenger hunt like they did every month, with modifications for safety. This time all staffers would be out in the woods to stand guard, not just the counselors whose cabins were competing. They were going to set up a big screen and a projector out on the lake too, so the wolflings could float on inner tubes and watch a movie. He'd already made arrangements to rent a floating screen and projector from a place in Bloomington. The inflatable obstacle course had looked like fun, but he didn't want to risk an overexcited wolfling popping claws.

Wolflings trickled into the auditorium for Harris's next class, so Scott gave him an awkward bro hug and left. Harris usually would have made fun of him for it, but they all needed the contact today. All of the wolflings were hanging out in clusters, draped all over each other at every opportunity. Intimacy and physical affection would calm their nerves, and sharing their scents would help their wolves. Camp H.O.W.L. and the other Turn camps were some of the only places teens were actively encouraged to get physical with each other. It was why their first day included orientation and a sex-ed lecture. Many of the wolflings would never progress to that level of intimacy at camp, but they wanted to make sure those who did were safe.

Harris waited a few more minutes for the last of his students to arrive. They were all there before the official start time, probably because they weren't allowed to mill around outside.

"This is the second class in our series about Werewolfing in the Community," he said, grinning when a few wolflings snickered. "I know, it's a ridiculous name. But that's exactly what you'll be doing for the rest of your lives. Unless you choose to live on a secluded island or bunk up at one of the werewolf communal ranches out in Montana and Utah, you'll be living under scrutiny every day of your lives."

The faces in front of him ran the gamut from bored to terrified. He hated scaring the wolflings, but it was a necessary evil. They were nineteen—the impulse control part of their brains was still essentially goo. Unfortunately, they were going to have to grow up fast now that they'd gone through the Turn.

"Dr. Perry talked about social media last week, and I know you all thought it was funny, but he was dead serious when he said a careless Snap or Instagram post could out all of Were society. It's why we have such stringent rules about what you can and can't post. But we also have to figure out how to pass for human in the real world, and that has even more challenges."

"We've been human all our lives," Stephanie said with a sneer. "I think we can handle it."

Harris took a breath and counted to ten in his head, holding her stare. When she looked away, he relaxed. She was still trying to flex her muscles at camp, but she wasn't nearly as dangerous as Harris had assumed that first day.

"Thank you for volunteering, Ms. Chastain. Adam, Sam, Jennifer, come on up with Stephanie. We're going to do some role-playing."

Everyone groaned, but he was sure this was secretly their favorite part of the seminar. It got them up and out of their seats, and even if they felt silly repeating rules back to each other and playing out scenarios, it was less boring and more effective than lecturing.

"For the sake of this exercise, we're going to say we're on a platform waiting for a train," he said when the four of them came up. "Stephanie, you're in front.

Everyone else, I want you to crowd in around her. Really get up in her space like someone would on a crowded platform. The next train is coming, and you're all late for work. You can't miss it. You shoulder up next to her to get a good position."

Harris used his body to add to the fray, pushing up until his shoulder was right in Stephanie's face. Jennifer gave her a little push, which sent her straight into Adam, who didn't budge. Sam shuffled in closer, his chin almost touching the top of her head.

A growl tore from Stephanie's throat, and her eyes flashed amber. Harris reached out and put a hand on her shoulder, squeezing it.

"All right everyone, thanks. Go sit down." Stephanie glared at him but stayed where she was, since he was still holding on to her.

"Sometimes we get into physical situations that are uncomfortable. Your wolf processes that as danger, and as you can all see, we're at higher risk for shifting when our wolves feel like they're cornered."

"That's not what a train platform is really like, though," Stephanie said, jaw set into a defiant clench.

"No, it's not. But you will run into a situation like that at some point in your life, I guarantee it. A concert, a Black Friday sale, a crowded train station because the last two trains were out of service and everyone is antsy to get home."

He squeezed Stephanie's shoulder again and motioned for her to take her seat. She bolted for it.

"Now, what Stephanie did, flashing her eyes, is a pretty low-level reaction. She did a great job not shifting under the discomfort. That's something we'll be practicing in small groups, but we'll wait until next week for that."

The exercise bore too much resemblance to being herded into the bunkers, so Harris figured they should skip it for now. The wolflings cheered, and Harris grinned, shaking his head.

"You're not getting out of group work that easily," he told them. He held up a box of canisters. "Another thing you need to be in complete control of are your reactions. You're faster and stronger than you were before the Turn, so obviously you have to work on keeping that in check when you're with humans. What else along those lines do you need to worry about?"

Candice's hand shot up, and Harris called on her, pleased to see that yesterday's craziness hadn't caused her to retreat back into her shell around her fellow wolflings.

"Our senses," she said. "It's harder to pretend we don't hear or smell things."

He beamed at her. "Exactly. It will be starker when you go home, since this is an unfamiliar place and you have nothing to compare it to. But at home, you'll find you're able to scent your parents' emotions, hear your coworkers when they're in other rooms—all sorts of things."

A movement at the back of the room caught his eye, and Harris looked up, startled to see Jackson standing near the door. He slipped into a seat and motioned for Harris to continue.

He'd lost his train of thought completely. What had they been talking about? "Anyone else have an example?"

"We'll hear our neighbors having sex," Adam yelled out, and giggles erupted in the room.

Right. He'd been talking about the importance of pretending to have human senses. He was an expert on that, since he'd successfully ignored the fact that Jackson had smelled like arousal around him for years. Chemosignals weren't the same thing as consent, which was something he'd address with the wolflings in a later class. Harris knew he was attractive, and as a result a lot of strangers and even friends smelled like arousal around him. As he smelled around every reasonably attractive person who caught his eye. It didn't mean anything deeper than an appreciation of the other's appearance. Unless the person addressed it or flirted, it was just background noise.

"Yes," he said, rolling his eyes. "That too. We're going to talk about chemosignals later, but for now let's split up and get some practice ignoring a pungent scent."

He handed Emma the box of canisters. "These all have scents that are designed to be distracting. I want each member of your group to take turns having a normal conversation with the group and continue to talk as if nothing is wrong after the canister is opened. The goal here is to practice playing human while your supernatural senses are running amok."

The class split into their groups, and Jackson made his way down to the desk.

"Hey. Missed you this morning," Harris said, trying to sound casual.

Jackson opened his mouth to respond, but a wolfling dropped a canister across the room. It rolled down the steps and everyone started sneezing as the scent permeated the air. It had been full of pine-scented air freshener beads and now they were everywhere.

Thank God. He didn't need his love life playing out in front of a roomful of wolflings.

Harris shot Jackson an apologetic look. "Sorry, I've got to go deal with this. Did you need something?"

Jackson hesitated before shaking his head. "I'll catch you after class."

Harris nodded. "You can walk me over to the mess. I've got duty there after this."

He headed over to clean up the mess instead of watching Jackson leave. The wolflings were all rubbing their noses.

"This is what I'm talking about," Harris said, sweeping at a clump of beads with his shoe. He'd need a broom to get them all, but the smell would be bearable if he got most of them back in the canister.

"What you're all doing right now? Holding your noses, coughing—a human wouldn't be doing that. The smell wouldn't be strong enough to elicit that kind of response. You've got to train yourself *not* to react."

"So, we're supposed to pretend our noses aren't burning?"

Harris looked up, pinpointing a boy at the back of the room. "Yes, Liam, that's exactly what you're supposed to do. That's literally the entire point of this exercise."

Harris sighed and stood up, the half-full canister tucked under his arm. "Did you see me covering my nose? Do you think the smell was any less strong for me? It wasn't. But I didn't allow myself to react."

He waved a hand out at the kids, who had all taken their seats again. "We can't do much about the pure physiological reactions. The sneezing and coughing? That's out of our control. But you can pass it off as a dry throat or a patch of dust—humans will always believe the easiest answer."

Just like friends will kindly overlook your all-encompassing crush on them until they decide it's beneficial for them and indulge you long enough to get you into bed. Harris squashed the thought and focused back on the class. Several of them had pulled their shirts up over their noses, and others were hiding their faces in the crooks of their arms.

They were drama queens. It wasn't bad enough to merit that. Harris was tempted to borrow the pepper spray Drew carried around with him for safety. *That* would teach them a lesson.

"Even though humans operate on the Occam's razor principle—the most common explanation is probably the answer—you still have to have ironclad control out in public. We give you a good foundation for that, but you're going to have to keep working at it at home until your Alpha agrees you're ready."

He looked at the clock. "We'll end a few minutes early so you can escape the smell. But be prepared for small group work tomorrow! We're going to keep doing drills until you can manage to hide your reactions."

A few of the wolflings grumbled as they walked out, but most just bolted for the doors without comment. He was going to have to have someone come help him work on toning down their speed and agility so they walked like humans.

Harris dragged his heels cleaning up the mess, but a few minutes after the last wolfling left, Jackson poked his head in the door.

"Class over?"

Harris nodded. "I hate having the slot before dinner. They're too hungry to concentrate on anything but the clock."

Jackson laughed. "I remember those days."

The Turn took a lot of energy, as did shifting. The wolflings were burning through an incredible amount of energy right now, and it showed in their eating habits.

Harris would have to text George to come clean the room. They were going to let the wolflings watch a movie in here later, and he didn't want to have to deal with all the bitching over the pine scent.

Jackson reached out and touched his elbow as Harris stared at the desk and ran through the mental list of things he had to do tonight.

He looked up, his stomach dropping at the expression on Jackson's face. This was going to hurt.

Jackson rubbed his neck. "I got the call from the Tribunal."

Harris had been preparing himself for this, but it still ripped the air out of his lungs. "So soon?"

"It's only a week short of their estimate. They need a fully functional team. It's already been over a month since the position opened up. I'd imagine the team is more than ready to be back at full steam."

Of course. Harris tried to take a breath, but his chest wouldn't cooperate. He coughed to cover the awkwardness, forcing himself to inhale.

"They offered you the job, I assume?"

Jackson nodded, but his smile didn't quite reach his eyes.

"That's wonderful," Harris said, ducking his head to hide the tears that clouded his vision. "It's—wow. Just what you wanted. Wonderful. I said that already, didn't I? I mean, congrats. Really. I have to get to a session, but—wow. Yeah. That's great."

He fled before Jackson gave him any more details. Honestly, Harris didn't want any. Jackson wasn't his anymore—he was the Tribunal's. The sooner Harris got that through his head the better.

Jackson called his name, but Harris pretended he hadn't heard him and pushed through the double doors. Thank God for the restrictions—there weren't any groups of wolflings out on the lawn or milling around outside the building. Harris let the tears stream down his face as he took off at a sprint. He was supposed to be supervising dinner in the mess, but he just wanted to curl up and lick his wounds.

He hadn't had his phone all day, since he'd left it charging next to his bed this morning. Harris cursed. He'd meant to go get it a dozen times today, but something had always come up. Part of him knew he'd been hiding from possible text messages from Jackson, but the absurdity of that almost made him laugh now. Bad news had a way of finding you whether or not you had your phone.

"Hey, man. It's taco night, what are you doing out here?"

Harris swallowed hard and looked up, catching sight of Scott a few yards away. Scott did a double take when he came closer.

"Harris? What's wrong?"

Harris shook his head. "Stuff. Personal stuff. Find someone to cover for my mess duty? And have Anne Marie cancel my evening sessions."

Scott reached out but let his hand hover over Harris's shoulder, like he wasn't sure if his touch would be welcomed. Harris offered him a weak smile.

"Of course. But are you sure you don't need someone with you? Harris, man, you look—"

Harris had a good idea of what he must look like right now. He cut Scott off with a shake of his head. "I'm good. Tell her I'll be fine for tomorrow, okay? I just need the night off."

Scott pursed his lips but nodded and jogged off toward the mess. Harris took a shuddery breath and tried to think clearly.

He had no idea if Jackson was going to come after him or not, but his cabin would be the first place he checked. Same with his office, so he turned toward the lake. No one was allowed to be out, so the wolflings wouldn't be using the boats tonight. He'd hole up in the boathouse. It was kind of poetic, given that had been the scene of their first date.

Harris muffled a sob against his arm. He was an idiot. He'd known this would hurt, but he hadn't realized how much. Would it have been better if they'd had a week together, like he'd planned? Or would it have been worse?

The boathouse was locked, but he balanced on the thin ledge the wainscoting formed and made his way around to the side where he could jump onto the dock.

Harris climbed into a canoe tied up in one of the slips. There was a pontoon boat with padded seats in the other slip, but Harris wasn't looking for comfort right now. He curled up on the floor of the canoe and closed his eyes, focusing on the way the boat swayed in the water.

He'd take a nap. He always advised his patients hiding from your problems never worked, but it wouldn't hurt to try for a little bit.

Chapter Twelve

JORDAN tapped at his phone, broadcasting his annoyance loud and clear with his brusque movements.

"If your flight is at eight we're already going to be cutting it close."

Jackson growled, sending yet another text to Harris. He'd been too stunned by Harris's reaction to the news to follow him out of the auditorium, and by the time he'd gone after him Harris had been nowhere to be found. He'd even tried to follow his scent, but the camp was so saturated with it the trails were difficult to pick out.

"I know, I know. But I need to talk to him before I leave."

Jordan frowned at him. "If he told you to take the job, then take the job. Maybe you're reading too much into things. We know he's into you, but he might not be looking for something long-term. I mean, his life is here at the camp. Are you telling me you'd be happy living here?"

Jackson wouldn't be. But he didn't have to—he could stay in Lexington and keep his spot on the force. Between that and Fang and Fury, he'd be happy. Or at least, he would if it meant being with his mate. They might not be able to live together, but at least he'd see him on the weekends.

He'd been so sure Harris was all in after last night, but the way he'd brushed him off earlier made him doubt his senses. Maybe they *hadn't* connected the way he'd thought they had during sex. It might have been his imagination, or how much he wanted it to be true. If they really were mates, Harris would fight for him, wouldn't he? He wouldn't be content to let Jackson walk away.

"We can't wait anymore. You can keep trying to call him from the car." Jordan wrapped an arm around Jackson's shoulders and steered him toward the garage.

Jackson had called the Tribunal recruiter that afternoon to decline the job, but she'd insisted he come meet with the Enforcers face-to-face. It would make it a lot harder to turn the job down, but how could he take it when it meant giving up a life with Harris?

He relented and let Jordan put him in the car. "I don't understand why he won't pick up. He didn't let me explain. He just… took off."

Jordan started the SUV. "Well, you'd just told him you were offered a job across the country. What did you want him to say?"

"That he wanted me to stay," Jackson blurted.

Jordan gave him a long look as he waited for the gates to open. "And what did you say when Raoul asked you not to apply?"

Jackson looked down at the phone in his lap. Still no message from Harris. "That I wasn't going to give up my career for a relationship."

"And then you broke up with him," Jordan said. "Can you see how Harris might have gotten the impression you were dumping him?"

Jackson groaned and slammed his head back against the headrest. "Fuck."

"Yeah, buddy," Jordan said. "This is a shitshow of your own making. I don't blame him for ignoring you. Give him some time. At some point, he'll read your texts and realize you're only flying out to New York to turn down the job. I'm sure he'll call you then."

But would he be calling to tell Jackson not to do it? He had no way of knowing if Harris wanted him to take the job or not. If he took what Harris said at face value, then he should accept it. But Harris hadn't looked happy. The smile he'd given him had been brittle at best. Jackson would know for sure if the scent of the damn pine air freshener hadn't drowned out Harris's chemosignals, but as it was he was flying blind.

"I'm going to do it," he said decisively. "This isn't what I want. Even if Harris hates me, I'll turn it down and come back here to convince him he's my mate."

Jordan chuckled. "That's not really how it works."

"How would you know? You don't have a mate," Jackson snapped. "It took me how many years to realize Harris was mine? That just means he needs time. Maybe he hasn't realized it yet. But I wouldn't be able to form a mating bond with him if we weren't compatible."

"Being compatible doesn't mean you're mates. And even if you are, it's not like set in stone. You could have dozens of potential mates out there, Jacks. We're not real wolves. We have free will, and that means the ability to walk away from something even if your biology is pushing you toward it."

He knew that. Fuck, it was all he'd been able to think about for weeks. But he had to try. He'd spent so much time trying to deny it or figure out how to work around it—but last night had proven that they belonged together. He'd been fooling himself trying to ignore it.

Jordan sighed and looked over at him. "You've already formed a bond. This isn't hypothetical."

Jackson grimaced. "I'm almost positive I felt him last night. It's not just a fledgling bond. I think we've completed all the steps except for the formal mating."

He rolled his eyes when Jordan let out a whistle. "Damn, boy, you move fast."

Actually, he moved slowly. Glacially slowly. This bond must have been forming for a decade. He was just finally at a place in his life he could acknowledge it.

"What about your career? You always said you weren't going to let anything stop you from being a Pack Second."

"I still want that. But I think I can have it and still have my mate. Maybe it pushes the timeline out, sure. But Harris won't want to stay at Camp H.O.W.L. forever. And when he's ready to move on, we can try to find a Pack that needs me."

It would likely be a small Pack in the middle of nowhere and not a big-city Pack like he'd planned, but that didn't matter. It would work out.

Jordan started to say something but snapped his mouth shut, shaking his head. "You do you, buddy. But have you talked to Drew about this? Your dad? Anyone?"

He was talking to Jordan now, but he didn't think that was the answer Jordan was looking for. "I will."

"Before you commit career suicide or after?"

Jackson clenched his fist around his phone. "After."

"So, you're not disputing this is a terrible idea?"

He wasn't. But he honestly didn't see any other path. He'd wanted this job for so long, and he felt sick giving it up, but he felt worse when he thought about being forced to sever his mating bond.

"Good talk," he said, learning forward and turning the radio up to end the conversation.

JACKSON'S flight arrived twenty minutes early, so he had time before the car from the Tribunal arrived to pick him up. He didn't have any luggage because he didn't plan to stay. He had a late afternoon flight back to Indiana, and with any luck he'd be with his mate by dinner.

He slumped on a bench and took out his phone. Harris hadn't returned any of his calls or texts while he'd been in the air. He blew out a breath and called Drew, who answered on the second ring like he'd been waiting for a call. Jackson felt like an asshole—he'd been calling to see if his stepbrother knew anything about Harris, completely forgetting he'd promised to let him know the moment he landed.

"Get there okay?"

"Yeah. Waiting for my ride now." Jackson fiddled with the zipper on his bookbag. "Hear anything from Harris?"

"He didn't text you before he left?"

Jackson's stomach dropped to his toes. "He *left*?"

"Just to take Candice to Bloomington," Drew said in a rush, clearly picking up on Jackson's distress. "She has a meeting with her agent today, and Harris volunteered to take her because he had to go into town to get that inflatable movie screen thing. They left just after breakfast. He said they'd be back this afternoon."

Jackson took a breath. "Have you talked to him?"

"No. The idiot spent the night in the boathouse, I guess. Andrew found him there when he opened it up this morning. He slept in one of the canoes. Did you guys have a fight?"

Everything had happened in such a whirlwind he hadn't told Drew about spending the night with Harris or how they'd parted yesterday. Hell, he hadn't even told him he was turning down the Enforcer job.

"Something like that."

He'd called for advice, but the request died on his tongue. Jackson didn't need Drew's counsel on this. He already knew what he had to do—he just had to dig deep and find the courage to do it.

"Hey, I've got to go," he said as a black town car pulled up in front of the curb. "Thanks."

"For what?"

"For picking up the phone." Jackson grabbed his bookbag and stood up. "My ride's here."

"Good luck."

Jackson grinned. He had a mate and a life to start— he already had all the luck he needed.

THE news hadn't gone over well, but Jackson was still smiling ear-to-ear when he left the Tribunal headquarters. He'd accomplished what he came to New York to do, even though it was difficult. The Tribunal put on a full court press to get him to stay, offering him more money and the opportunity to be on a fast track toward being a team lead with the Enforcers. It was everything he could have hoped for, but he still felt like he was on top of the world walking away from it.

That had to prove they were really mates, didn't it? He'd just slammed a door shut he'd been working years to open, and he didn't have the slightest regret.

"Leaving already, sir?" the guard at the reception desk asked when Jackson walked up.

"It was a short meeting," Jackson said, flashing him a smile. He handed over the laminated ID badge he'd been given when he arrived, waiting as the guard opened a lock box to return his phone and bookbag.

The Tribunal had an impressive security setup. He had a pang of regret at all the things he could have learned here, but it was fleeting. He was getting the better deal in the end. Even if he had to spend the rest of his life with the Lexington police force, he'd have Harris there with him.

"Have a good day, Enforcer Berrings," the man said as he handed over his things.

It wasn't a title he had a right to anymore, since they'd stripped his district Enforcer duties after he'd declined the Tribunal job. He'd hoped he could keep it, but he understood why they did it. He'd have more time to spend at Camp H.O.W.L. this way, at least.

Jackson thumbed across his phone, frowning when he saw dozens of missed calls and even more missed texts. He leaned up against the outside of the building, staring at his phone. None of the notifications were from Harris.

"Jackson!" He nearly dropped his phone, startled by the frantic voice.

Tate ran toward him, flagging him down. "Jackson," he called again, out of breath. He stopped in front of him, his scent sour with panic and his expression solemn. "They've been trying to get a hold of you. Harris is missing."

Jackson frowned. "He went into Bloomington with Candice—"

"They know. But he didn't come back. Candice was supposed to meet with her agent for an hour, tops. They should have been back at Camp H.O.W.L. hours ago, and when Jordan tracked the car, he saw it hadn't moved."

Terror washed over him. He should be able to do something—anything—but his limbs were like concrete, and he couldn't think straight.

"Jordan said there were some strange scents by the car. Candice's agent confirmed she never made it to the meeting. They think someone snatched them off the street."

Oh God. This wasn't just the paparazzi—this was something different.

"The FBI?"

"They don't have them. Since there's no evidence of foul play, they won't open a kidnapping case for at least twenty-four hours."

Of course. Because they couldn't tell them that the crime scene *smelled* funny. Jackson reached for the fledgling bond inside him and felt nothing. That wasn't out of the ordinary—the only time he'd been able to feel Harris was when they'd been in bed together the previous night, and even that was shaky. It was a new bond, and it wasn't complete—he'd have to be close to even try to pull at it. He certainly couldn't do it from hundreds of miles away.

"I've got to get to Bloomington," Jackson rasped out.

His flight wasn't for a few hours. Harris and Candice might be dead by then. If they weren't already. *Stop*, he scolded himself. This was what he had trained for. Just because the victim was his mate didn't mean he couldn't work this like a case. He needed to stay calm and *think*.

He'd worked several kidnappings as a regional Enforcer—

Fuck.

"I've got to get them to help," he said, pushing off the wall and heading back to the glass doors he'd come out of minutes ago. "They have to help. They can fly a team to Bloomington and be on the ground faster than I could get there."

Jackson took off, leaving Tate standing on the sidewalk. The guard reached for his weapon when Jackson ran back through the doors. He was sure he looked deranged.

"My mate has been kidnapped. I need to talk to Enforcer Abernathy. She can authorize a team to deploy to the scene."

The guard shook his head. "Sir, that's not—"

Jackson slammed his hands on the desk. "We're wasting time! Call Abernathy!"

The guard pressed a button on his collar, calling for backup. Fuck. He had to get to Harris. He didn't have time for this shit.

Thirty seconds later four more guards burst through a door, weapons drawn on Jackson. He put his hands up, trying his best not to look threatening. He wouldn't be able to help Harris if he was in a Tribunal cell.

The elevator dinged a second later, and Enforcer Abernathy and one of the Tribunal Alphas exited. She looked startled for a moment, then gathered herself and strode over, taking in the scene.

"What's going on here? Mr. Berrings is not a threat. Stand down." She looked at the guard who'd been manning the desk. "Fellowes, what happened?"

"He left and came back a few minutes later yelling about a kidnapping. He's unhinged, ma'am."

Her eyes narrowed as she studied Jackson. "Speak, Berrings."

Thank fuck. "Respectfully, I came back asking for help. When I left the building, I found out that my mate and a high-profile wolfling from Camp H.O.W.L. were abducted during my absence. I need to get back to Bloomington before the trail goes cold. I was hoping you would dispatch a team."

She looked at the Tribunal Alpha, who nodded. They'd have figured out he was talking about Candice.

"We'll take this to the Tribunal. Most are still here. If they agree, we can be wheels up in twenty. Berrings, I assume you want a ride?"

Chapter Thirteen

HIS head was throbbing. The first thing Harris noticed when he woke up was the pain radiating from the back of his head. He tried to swallow, his mouth so dry it felt like his tongue had swollen to twice its size.

What the fuck happened?

He struggled to sit up, but his hands slipped on the cool floor. Cement? He ran his fingertips over it. Definitely not the floor of his cabin. The only building on campus that had a cement floor was the garage, but this was too dim for that. The headache blurred his vision, and he strained to make out his surroundings.

He heard heartbeats, but none of them were in his immediate vicinity. Waking up alone and confused was becoming a disturbing habit.

Harris eased up on his elbow, fighting off the wave of nausea that hit him when he raised his head. He touched the nape of his neck gingerly, grimacing when his hand came away wet. The copper tang of blood was heavy in the air. Even with his foggy brain he could put two and two together. He'd been hit with something, probably knocked out. The fuzziness was likely a concussion.

He probed at the base of his skull again, wincing as pain lanced through him. The cut had healed, but his hair was matted with blood, and he had one hell of a bump.

How long had he been out? The blow must have cracked his skull. That would have taken considerable time to heal.

The last thing he remembered was parking the car and telling Candice he'd walk her to her meeting. Fuck. Candice.

His head spun as he forced himself up. He had to find Candice. She might be hurt. He still had no idea where he was, so he didn't dare call out to her, but he leaned against a cinder-block wall, closed his eyes, and focused all his energy on his hearing.

There was a heartbeat on the other side of the thick wall and one somewhere in front of him—a few dozen yards, maybe. He thought he could make out a few more in the distance, but they were indistinct. It could have been one person or five.

What would Jackson do in a situation like this? Harris almost snorted out a laugh at the thought of Jackson letting himself get kidnapped. He'd never fuck up this badly. Harris had been distracted, nursing his broken heart, and he and Candice had been kidnapped because of it.

The first thing Jackson would do was assess the situation. Harris pretended the voice in his head was Jackson's, and he let it guide him. It was comforting to have his mate there with him, even if it was in his imagination.

Harris took a breath and opened his eyes. The dim room had stopped spinning, but he was still having trouble focusing. He used the wall as a guide and shuffled forward. There was a metal grate across one wall. Hinged like it extended from the ceiling. Was he in some sort of cell? He turned around, scanning the space. It was smaller than he'd originally thought and empty. This wasn't an official cell; that much was for sure. He'd gotten familiar with the jail-issue toilet and uncomfortable regulation cot at the sheriff's station.

He peered through the metal grate. A bank of similar cells lined the wall across from him, and farther down he saw a forklift.

He was in a warehouse. This must be a storage bay. He worked his fingers into the grate and tried to tug it up, but it wouldn't budge. He squinted and saw a padlock on the outside. Fuck.

"Hello?" The whisper was barely more than an exhalation, and Harris moved to the edge of the cell, his ear pressed against the grate.

"Candice?" he whispered back.

She sobbed quietly. "Oh my God, Dr. Wick. I thought they killed you! There was so much blood."

"Are you all right? Did they hurt you?"

"No."

His knees went weak with relief. "Good. That's good."

She sobbed again, her heartbeat fluttering. He had to calm her down before they attracted attention. Harris extended his fingers as far as he could through the grate. "Can you see my fingers? Focus on my fingers. I'm fine, see?"

He cursed when he realized he'd extended the hand that had his blood on it, but Candice seemed comforted by it anyway. Her panicked breathing slowed, and her heart rate followed.

"Good," he crooned. "Can you tell me anything you've noticed about this place? Are there guards? Did you see who took us?"

"Th-they were blue," she stammered. "Not like blue-blue, but their skin had a weird bluish tinge. They looked like humans, but sharper, maybe? Meaner. They didn't smell right. Some of them had swords and other had these pointy stick things. I didn't see any guns, so we can fight them, right?"

Fuck. Harris closed his eyes and rested his head on the grate. Fae. They'd been kidnapped by the motherfucking fae.

"We're not trained to fight," he said quietly, hoping she didn't question him further. They stood no chance against the Fae Guard.

"What are they?" she asked. "Are we going to die?"

Probably.

"No, of course not," he said, careful to keep the tremor out of his voice.

"Liar," another voice called. "You were dead the minute they took you."

Harris raised his head and squinted into the gloom. The speaker was in the bay across from his, but he could barely make him out. "Richard?"

"They're trying us for exposure," Richard said. He snorted. "It's all that little bitch's fault."

Harris curled his fingers around the grate, claws sprouting. "None of this is Candice's fault. *You* were the one who sold your story to the press. If this is anyone's fault, it's yours."

The Fae Council was the ultimate supernatural authority. They were stronger and older than any other supernatural race, and they'd taken it upon themselves centuries ago to protect the supernatural world from exposure. The council kept up the veneer of civility by having "trials," but Harris had never heard of anyone being acquitted for a crime the Fae Council accused them of. They were swift and brutal. The punishment was always death.

"Have they given judgment yet?"

"No," Richard answered, his bravado fading. "They're arranging to have the selkie released into their custody. When they have her, they'll move forward with the trial."

That was good. It bought them a little time at least. It probably wouldn't help them in the long run, but there was a first time for everything.

"Dr. Wick? What is he talking about? What trial? Where are we?"

Harris took a calming breath to ensure his voice didn't waver. He didn't want to scare her. "The Fae Council is in charge of keeping all supernaturals a secret. When there's been a breach, they often intervene. They usually leave Weres and shifters alone because our own Tribunal polices exposure incidents very well. I'm sure this is just a misunderstanding. The Tribunal will come for us."

Richard snorted again but didn't say anything. *His* fate was sealed either way. Both councils would give him the death penalty for his betrayal. But Candice hadn't done anything wrong, and neither had he.

"I'm sorry," Candice said, her voice thick with
tears. "It's my fault. If I hadn't asked to go meet with
my agent, we'd still be safe at Camp H.O.W.L."

He didn't want to tell her that if the fae wanted
them, they'd get them no matter where they were. The
reports of staffers feeling like they were being watched
made a lot more sense. The fae could hide their scent
and make themselves virtually invisible. They'd been
stalking them. The camp's defenses would be child's
play to a Fae Guard.

"No, sweetheart. I'm the adult here. If I thought
there was the slightest risk, I wouldn't have brought
you. Even Jordan thought we'd be okay, and he's our
security specialist." Harris slid down the wall and
rested his aching head against it. "Why don't you try to
get some sleep? It's got to be late."

Truthfully, he had no idea how much time they'd
spent in the warehouse. The little rooms had no natural
light, and his concussion was messing with his body
clock. But it couldn't hurt to sleep. He wanted to
manage her trauma the best he could, and getting her
to lie down and check out for a bit was the best way to
do that.

"You'll still be here when I wake up?"

His heart broke at how young and vulnerable she
sounded. "Of course."

He hated himself for the lie, but reassuring her was
more important than telling her the truth. He had no idea
if he'd be there or if he'd be taken away as she slept.
The Fae Guard had all the power here. All he could do
was sit and hope his mate would come for him.

Chapter Fourteen

JACKSON leaned his head against the cool glass of the helicopter's window. They were twenty minutes out from Bloomington, and he had to fight the urge to jump out so he could run. About two hours into their flight, he'd started feeling flashes of panic that weren't his. Intermittent and faint, like a voice through a bad phone connection.

The sense of fear and unease had gotten stronger the closer they got to Indiana. Tate had reassured him it was a good thing—it meant Harris was still alive. But it also meant he was in danger, and Jackson was having a hell of a time containing his wolf, knowing his mate was reaching out to him, scared.

He jumped when Tate squeezed his elbow.

"You'll find him," Tate shouted, the words almost lost to the sound of the rotors. The helicopter the Enforcers used was a modified military transport, unlike any of the commercial helicopters Jackson had been in. They were making good time, but it wasn't big on amenities like insulation or doors.

It was designed to make it easier for the Enforcers to get on the ground efficiently. He wondered if they'd be dropped off six feet above the ground or if the pilot would land because of the civilians on board. He looked at the Enforcers, all clad in their tactical gear, holding on to straps on the ceiling instead of sitting down.

Enforcer Abernathy hadn't wanted Tate along, but Tate insisted. Harris was one of his closest friends, so Jackson understood. If the tables were turned and the Enforcers had ordered *him* to stay in New York while they launched a rescue mission, things would have gotten hairy fast. The way Tate had held his ground against an intimidating group had been admirable.

In the end, they'd let him come because they didn't have the time to waste arguing with him. Jackson hoped they didn't regret it. Tate wasn't trained in tracking or combat, so he'd be dead weight. Maybe he'd stay in the helicopter with the pilot. That would get him close to the action but keep him safe. Harris would never forgive him if he let Tate get killed.

"Five minutes!"

Everyone straightened at the pilot's words. Jackson stood, gripping a strap from the ceiling. His tennis shoes weren't ideal for jumping out of a helicopter, but they'd have to do.

"We'll be landing at a helipad at the airport. I want everyone strapped in!"

The Enforcers moved with eerie grace and precision, taking seats and buckling themselves in. Jackson sat back down, his knees already shaky. He could feel Harris like a solid presence now, taking up room in his head. He'd be able to find him, but it might take hours. The bond didn't give him a picture of where Harris was; it just gently tugged at him.

"You gonna be able to do this, Berrings?"

Jackson looked up at Enforcer Abernathy, who had settled into the seat across from his.

"Yes, ma'am."

She didn't look convinced but nodded. "I've got a Glock for you, and there are more weapons in the cache. Help yourself to whatever you're comfortable using." She offered Tate an apologetic smile. "Sorry, Dr. Lewis, you're here for transport only. You don't have the training or experience to join us on the mission."

Thank fuck. That was one less thing for Jackson to worry about. He shot her a grateful smile, happy that she'd taken that off his plate. Jackson would have put his foot down, but it was better if Abernathy played the heavy in this.

"I can—"

She shook her head. "Negative. We don't take civilians into the field with us. You're welcome to stay with the helicopter. After the extraction, we'll be flying on to Camp H.O.W.L. Perhaps you can be of use with calming the victims."

Jackson bristled but forced himself to keep his mouth shut. It was such a cold, clinical way of viewing things. Harris and Candice weren't just *victims*. They deserved to be named. But he'd been guilty of the same thing countless times as a cop. It was easier to distance yourself emotionally if you didn't use names.

"We've got intel that traces fae movement in the area. I think there's a good chance that's who has them."

Jackson had to look away, tears stinging his eyes. The fae were vicious. If they were the kidnappers, this was going to be messy. Not impossible, but not pretty.

"Are you going to be able to separate yourself enough to help with this mission?"

Jackson swallowed hard and looked Abernathy in the eye, nodding. "We'll be able to use my mate bond to track them once we get close. You need me on the ground with you."

Abernathy's eyes were hard as she stared him down. He wondered if she'd ever been in love or had anyone she cared about more than her own life. Probably not, or she wouldn't be a top-level Enforcer.

"I can do it," he said, his eyes flashing at the unspoken challenge. "I'm a cop, first and foremost. I know how to compartmentalize. I realize protocol is to ban family members from working cases that involve a loved one, but there's literally no one else who could help you on this."

She nodded grudgingly. "One false move and you're gone. You're lucky you have two Alphas speaking on your behalf on the Tribunal. I didn't want to let you run the mission with us, but I was overruled."

That stunned Jackson. Two? His Alpha would, of course. But who was the second?

The helicopter came to a jolting stop, and he jumped up, more than ready to get out there. Hours had been lost while they were in transit, and he wasn't going to let another second slip by.

"Bring them back," Tate yelled over the noise of the rotors.

Jackson gave him a brief hug before jumping out and dashing away with the Tribunal team. There were two black SUVs on the tarmac, and he followed Abernathy to them.

Scott was sitting behind the wheel. He met Jackson's gaze with red-rimmed eyes.

"I'm so fucking sorry, man," he said when Jackson settled into the back seat, letting Abernathy take the front. Two other Enforcers crowded in with him. "We don't even know when they were taken. We didn't think to look for them until hours had passed."

"It's not your fault," Jackson said, his voice cracking.

"It truly isn't," Abernathy said. "If this is the work of the fae, there wasn't anything you could have done to prevent it. Likely they grabbed them here because it was convenient. If they wanted them, they'd have no trouble taking them no matter where they were."

Logically, Jackson agreed with her. The fae were slippery and smart, as well as being magically gifted. Nothing could keep them out if they were determined to get in. But the irrational part of him couldn't help but think if he'd been there this wouldn't have happened. If he'd woken Harris up yesterday morning instead of leaving him in an empty bed. If he'd forced him to stay and listen to him instead of letting Harris run away. If he'd canceled his trip when he hadn't been able to find Harris to tell him why he was going to New York.

"Do we have any leads about where they might be holding them?" Scott asked, heading out toward one of the main state roads.

"We don't track the fae, but we had a team out here recently tracking some Were separatists. They reported some unusual fae activity. They moved on because the separatists headed into Kentucky, but they were reasonably certain the fae had established a base of operations somewhere in Bloomington."

Bloomington was a large place. Jackson tried not to drown in discouragement. He needed to believe he could find Harris. The bond was so fragile that his stubborn insistence was all that was keeping it alive. So much of Were bondings were about intent, and Jackson intended to find Harris and confess how much he loved him. That was going to have to be enough to get him through this.

"They'll want an area that isn't high traffic," Abernathy said. "Fae mages are capable of glamours, but it takes a lot of energy to shield an entire building from human notice."

"They've been monitoring Camp H.O.W.L.," Jackson said. "We've had reports of people out on patrol feeling like they were being watched, strange noises in the forest, that sort of thing. Nothing registers on the security cameras."

Abernathy turned in her seat and gave him a grim smile. "They're very good at operating under the radar."

"Ma'am, I checked in with HQ, and the Fae Council has made contact with the Tribunal. They want us to hand over the selkie trespasser to be tried in their court."

"If they're sniffing around her, that's as good as confirmation they are the ones who took Harris and Candice. It was Candice's presence at Camp H.O.W.L. that attracted the selkie and prompted the FBI raid."

Jackson wanted to slam his fist through the window. Once again, his mate was in danger because *he* hadn't done his job right. Fuck.

"Calm yourself," Abernathy snapped. "You're not any good to anyone if you're going to be emotional."

How had he ever wanted to join the Enforcers? He never wanted to be that cold. Jackson would have to do his best to emulate her right now, though. He had to calm down so he could connect with Harris through the bond.

"I know it's hard, but we'll find them," Scott said, his voice so heartbreakingly earnest that Jackson's anger spiked again.

Scott had no idea how serious this was. And why would he? The fae were almost like a fairy tale to most Weres and shifters. They knew they existed, but most would go their entire lives without seeing one. The fae kept to themselves, except when they ventured out into the world to enact justice and put down people they perceived to be threats to the supernatural community. There was no way Scott could know being taken by the fae was a death sentence.

"I've got to figure out how to reach out to Harris through our mate bond. I'm not sure how to do it."

Scott half turned in his seat. "Aw, dude! You didn't tell me you'd bonded. Congratulations!" He was like a gigantic puppy.

"We haven't officially bonded yet. But there's a fledgling bond there—I could feel him when we were in the same room. I just have to figure out how to reach him over a longer distance and use it to figure out where he is."

It sounded ridiculous when he said it out loud. Mates who had been bonded for years couldn't feel each other outside a radius of a few feet, usually. It expanded as the bond matured, but to do what Jackson was trying—they'd need to have been mated for a decade at least.

"I can totally help with this," Scott said, excited. "Kayla's been working with me. First thing, close your eyes. Don't try to force yourself to breathe deeply. Just focus on the way your chest rises and falls naturally. Let the beating of your own heart center you. When you've calmed yourself enough to let your mind go blank, think about Harris and your intention to find him."

Jackson blinked. "Kayla has been working with you to feel a mate bond?"

Scott laughed. "No. She's been teaching me how to get into that headspace so we can have crazy-hot tantric sex, though."

Jackson snorted out a laugh. He'd walked right into that one. None of the Enforcers in the car even cracked a smile. More proof he'd made the right decision.

Jackson closed his eyes and tried to tune out the road noise and the heartbeats of everyone else in the car. He followed Scott's instructions, turning his focus inward. Jackson had no idea how much time was passing, but it seemed like the span of a blink before he could only hear his own steady breathing and the drum of his pulse.

He thought how delicious Harris looked curled up in his blanket burrito. About how he wanted always to be able to keep Harris as safe as he'd been in that moment, tucked up in blankets with mussed hair and an innocent smile.

He wanted to see that smile every morning for the rest of his life.

Jackson was almost startled out of his meditation when he felt a presence, like someone or something was standing behind him. It was familiar, but it was definitely distressed.

He strained toward it in his mind, but the more he reached for it, the fainter it became. Frustrated, he forced himself to ease back, letting the presence come to him. Images flitted through his mind, indistinct flutters of color that dispersed when he tried to look at them. It was like seeing something out of the corner of his eye, only to find it gone when he whirled around to look at it.

Jackson took another deep breath and stilled his mind, waiting for the next flash. This time he was ready for it, and he purposely did not turn his head toward it. He could make out vague images, but he wasn't sure what they meant. He tried again, but no images came.

"Is there an industrial district in Bloomington?" Jackson asked, blinking his eyes open. "Somewhere with a lot of factories and big warehouses?"

"What did you see? Were you able to connect with him?" Abernathy sounded flabbergasted.

"I don't know for sure, but I think so. He's scared, wherever he is. And I got images of cement floors and metal grates. I was thinking an abandoned factory or something. It's dark. There isn't much natural light at all."

"Did you see any guards?"

Jackson shook his head. "It's not like a movie. I only got snatches of vague images and feelings. He's hurt—I could tell that. And worried."

Scott made a U-turn. "There's an industrial park a few miles back. We'd passed close to it while you were meditating. Maybe he's there, and the proximity boosted the bond."

The industrial park was a cluster of older brick and limestone buildings. Most of their windows had been blacked out, either by the companies that had abandoned them or by squatters. Jackson's heart lurched when they drove closer.

"It's here. He's in one of these buildings."

"It would be helpful if you could tell us which one so we don't have to split into teams," Abernathy said, still sounding skeptical. "If we're walking into a fae hideout, we'll need significant backup."

Jackson scanned the buildings. "That one, I think," he said, pointing to a three-story building. "There wasn't much light, and that one has the fewest windows."

Scott pulled up short, stopping at the access road. "I'll get the SUV turned around and be waiting here," he said.

Abernathy nodded. She radioed the other car with her instructions, and soon they were all out, making their way carefully toward the abandoned warehouse.

"Eight heartbeats," one of the Enforcers said.

Abernathy held up a fist to stop them. "Team 1, move out around back to cover any potential exits. Team 2, you're with me. We're going in."

"How?" Jackson asked, studying the building. It looked impenetrable.

Abernathy grinned at him, looking engaged and interested for the first time. "Through the front door, of course."

She lifted her gun and checked it. Jackson did the same. It wasn't the standard-issue Glock he carried when he patrolled, but it was similar enough. It was a comforting, solid weight in his hand.

"Protocol F," she told her team. She looked at Jackson, lowering her voice. "We've trained for a fae confrontation, but I've never seen a fae in combat because—"

"Because no one ever survives to make a report," he finished for her.

She offered him another shit-eating grin. The woman was clearly bloodthirsty—a good trait to have on their side when going up against Fae Enforcers.

"They've never gone up against *my* team. We're good, Berrings. You get us there, and we'll get them out."

Or die trying. Jackson pushed that thought aside.

"Two waves," she said, motioning toward the door. "The victims are inside, location unknown. Getting them to safety is the top priority. Use force as needed. You have authorization to kill if necessary."

She drew several flashbangs out of her bag and handed them to the two Enforcers at the front of the line. "They'll enter with force and deploy these. They should stun anyone in the building, supernatural creatures included." She handed a pair of canisters to a third Enforcer. "The next line will use these. The smoke will obscure your view, but the contents won't affect anyone who isn't fae. For them, it causes weakness, numb limbs, confusion. It levels the playing field a bit. Then the team will subdue any downed fae through the usual means.

"Berrings, you're with me and the rest of the team. Once our scouts have cleared the way, we will enter and fan out to find the victims. You have authorization to defend yourself, but your mission is to find the hostages and lead them out."

Jackson gave her a brusque nod. He sent one last pulse of love through the bond before closing it down in his mind. He couldn't afford to be distracted in there. He'd have to trust his other senses to find Harris once they were in the building.

Abernathy gave the signal to move out, and the Enforcers wasted no time following it. The team jogged up to the doors, waiting while the first two broke them down and tossed in the flashbangs, followed by the smoke canisters.

He was in the rear, which was fine with him. Normally he liked being in the first wave of attack, but this was different. He swept in after the entryway was cleared, his eyes and nose stinging from the acrid smoke. He made his way deeper into the building, looking for any sign of the metal grates. The center of the warehouse was open, and he saw a pair of fae guarding the stairway to the second-floor corridor, which wound all the way around the building. Bingo.

He jumped up and caught the bottom of the metal walkway, then swung himself up. Enforcers had reached the stairs, and he ignored the sounds of fighting as he ran down the corridor, looking for any sign of Harris and Candice.

He stopped short when he smelled blood, his heart seizing. It was impossible to scent whose it was, thanks to the smoke filtering up from the first floor. Jackson pounded down the metal walkway, stopping in front of a grate that was dripping blood. A body sprawled across the cement floor inside, nearly sliced in half. Jackson steeled himself as he moved closer, giving a quick sob of relief when he recognized Richard, the staffer Anne Marie had fired.

Jackson gritted his teeth and moved on, looking into each of the gloomy cells. He glanced across the large room and saw movement in similar cell-like rooms on the other side.

The two sides connected with a catwalk-like corridor, and Jackson scrambled across it. He found Candice first, cowering in the back of her cell with her hands protecting her head.

Jackson rattled the grate. "Candice," he called lowly, not wanting to attract attention from the fae who were still fighting downstairs. "Candice, it's Jackson."

She tipped her head back, eyes widening when she saw him. She got up and ran to the grate, grabbing at his fingers.

"Dr. Wick is next door, and he's hurt," she said in a rushed whisper. "You've got to get him out first."

Jackson squeezed her fingers. "Let's get you out, and then I'll get him."

Every cell in his body was screaming at him to get Harris to safety, but Candice was the priority. She was a wolfling who had been entrusted to his care, and he didn't take that lightly. Neither did Harris. He knew his mate would kick his ass if he found out Jackson had left Candice there a moment longer than necessary.

Jackson spotted a padlock at the bottom of the grate. It attached the door to the metal floor. Fuck. Enforcer Abernathy probably had bolt cutters in her bag of tricks, but he had no idea where she was.

He looked around, gauging his options.

"Candice, get back in the corner and cover your head," he said. She scurried to obey, and as soon as she was in position he took aim and shot at the padlock. It took three tries, but it worked. It fell open, and he lifted the grate. She ran out of the cell and threw herself into his arms, clinging to him.

"It's okay," he said, patting her awkwardly. "Let's see if we can get Harris, okay?"

She let go of him, and he moved to the next room. Harris was sitting propped up against the wall, his pallor gray but his eyes open.

"You're so sexy when you shoot things," he rasped.

"Fuck off," Jackson managed to choke out. He couldn't afford to break down right now. The job wasn't done. He had to get Harris out of this damn cell and figure out how to get both of them out of here without wading into the fight downstairs.

"I love you too," Harris said. A trickle of blood ruined his otherwise angelic smile.

Shit. Was he bleeding internally? What had the fae done to him? Jackson had to know how badly he was injured before he could make a decision about what to do.

"Where are you hurt? Aside from your head, I mean."

Harris looked surprised, his hand raising to gingerly touch the back of his neck. "How did you know about my head?"

"The bond," Jackson said. "I felt it through the bond. It's how I found you. I don't know how much time we have. Where else are you hurt, baby?"

"My ribs," Harris answered. He tried to get up but fell back with a groan. "I think at least one is broken. Something's keeping it from healing. When the doors downstairs exploded, the guards went nuts. I think they killed Richard. One of them came for me with a spear but it hit my rib." He nodded toward the corner where a broken spear lay in a puddle of blood. "I pulled it out but I'm still not healing."

Jackson wanted to roar, but he pushed it down. He had to be strong for his mate right now. "Okay. I'll try to bind it when I get in there. Can you move away from the door? I had to shoot Candice's padlock off, but I can't do that if you're near it."

Harris tried to move again but let out a pained gasp. "I don't think I can."

Fuck. "That's okay. I'm going to get Candice out of here, and I'll be back for you. You stay there and try not to move."

Harris nodded before leaning his head back against the wall and shutting his eyes.

Leaving Harris there where he was still in danger felt like losing a limb, but he couldn't wait. He had to get Candice out. Jackson reached for his belt where he usually kept his radio when he was in uniform and cursed. He didn't have one. Abernathy hadn't had a spare.

He looked over the railing. Some of the fae were down, subdued by the gas and tied with magical restraints. But there were still two fighting the Enforcers. He couldn't take her down the stairwell.

"Candice, I'm going to put you on my back and we're going to go up, okay? Once we're on the roof I'll find us a way to climb down."

She nodded and put her arms around his neck. He boosted her so her legs wrapped around his waist.

"I'll be back, baby," he told Harris. "I love you."

"Love you too," Harris murmured, his words slurring.

Jackson jumped onto the railing, adjusting his balance to accommodate the weight on his back, and reached up to grasp the walkway above them. He didn't dare swing himself out to gain momentum this time, so he used his upper body to pull them up.

"Can you climb onto the walkway?"

Candice scrambled off him and onto the metal grating. Without her weight, he was easily able to pull himself up. He took her hand and ran toward the ladder to the roof. If he was lucky there would be a fire escape they could use to get down. If he was unlucky—well, a three-story fall wouldn't kill a Were. It would hurt like a bitch, and he'd probably break both legs carrying Candice, but he could do it.

He pushed Candice ahead of him, letting her go first. She darted up the ladder and burst out the trap door, her feet disappearing. He followed, breathing a sigh of relief when he saw the fire escape.

"Take that down to the ground and find Scott in the parking lot, okay? He has a radio. Tell him to let Abernathy know you're safe and that I went in to rescue Harris. Tell her I need bolt cutters on the second floor and a medic if she has one on her team."

Candice looked terrified but nodded. "I will."

He watched her clatter onto the fire escape before going back down the trap door. He jumped from the third-story railing, catching the railing on the floor below and swinging himself into the corridor.

Harris hadn't moved an inch in the five minutes he'd been gone. His chest was still rising and falling, but his breaths sounded pained.

"I'm here," he whispered. Harris's eyelids fluttered open, and the look of pure love and trust he gave Jackson made Jackson's heart hurt.

"You called me baby," Harris wheezed. "That's new."

Jackson scanned his surroundings looking for anything he could use to break the lock. "Would you prefer something else? My love? Sweetheart?"

Harris resettled himself against the wall, grimacing. "Mate."

Jackson swallowed hard. "Yes. Mate."

"'m sorry I never told you," Harris said, his words thick. "I didn't want to scare you."

Wait.

"Baby, why would you scare me? You're my mate. I'm the one who has been an asshole, denying it. And someday after I've made it up to you, maybe your wolf will accept me as its mate too."

Harris coughed, clutching at his ribs. "You've been my mate for years."

Footsteps clattered up the stairs before Jackson could answer. Abernathy appeared with a pair of bolt cutters.

"Good job getting the girl out," she said. "We've got all the guards subdued downstairs. Only one fatality."

Jackson didn't want to ask if it was theirs or the fae's. He had a feeling he wouldn't like the answer.

Abernathy clipped the padlock and raised the gate. "Scott radioed the camp. Your doctor was already en route. His ETA is ten minutes."

Jackson rushed into the cell as soon as the grate was open, falling to his knees in front of Harris. He took his hand carefully, worried any touch might hurt his ribs or cause further damage.

Another Enforcer appeared in the doorway, a black bag in his hands. He knelt on Harris's other side and pried his arm away from his ribs.

He snapped on a pair of gloves and cut Harris's bloodied T-shirt away, exposing a puncture wound that was still oozing blood.

The medic probed at it gently, drawing a hissed curse from Harris.

"Your rib is going to have to be set before you can heal," he said apologetically.

"Can it wait for Drew?" Jackson asked, watching them. "Would you be more comfortable if he did it?"

Harris groaned. "Just do it," he bit out.

The medic looked up at Jackson. "Can you hold him down? This will hurt like a bitch."

Chapter Fifteen

HARRIS didn't see why he had to spend the night in the infirmary. He'd healed up just fine after that sadistic bastard reached his hand inside and yanked on his broken rib. By the time Drew got there, the skin had knitted back together and his most pressing concern had been his concussion.

The ride back to Camp H.O.W.L. passed in a blur of pain and nausea. He'd lain across Drew's back seat with his head in Jackson's lap. Being that close to his mate sped his healing, which was an awesome benefit of a reciprocal mate bond he hadn't known about.

Jackson was conked out on a cot in the corner. He'd refused to leave Harris for a moment, which made Harris's wolf preen. He knew it was stupid—Jackson should have gone to grab a shower and rest somewhere more comfortable—but there was something about *seeing* his mate's devotion to him that was ridiculously satisfying.

His mate. Harris couldn't stop grinning. Jackson found them because he'd followed their bond. Harris wasn't going to say it made the horror show that was getting kidnapped by the fae worth it, but it kind of did. He hated that Candice was caught up in all of this. Watching Richard die hadn't been a walk in the park either, but honestly, it was the same fate he'd have gotten from the Tribunal.

Harris rubbed his side. His healing ribs ached a bit, but it was a small price to pay for being alive. The Fae Guard had intended to kill him, and he probably would have killed Candice as well if he hadn't gotten pulled into the fight downstairs with the Tribunal Enforcers. Harris wasn't sure what was going to happen to the fae who took them, but he couldn't say he cared. It was over, and he didn't want to dwell on it.

Not the healthiest outlook, and definitely one that would bite him in the ass later, but that was future Harris's problem. He could see why some of his patients refused to deal with their problems head-on.

A tentative knock sounded, and Candice eased the door open and poked her head inside.

"Is it okay to see you?"

He grinned and motioned her in. He pointed to Jackson and held a finger up to his lips. "Of course. Is Drew done checking you over?" he whispered.

She'd been whisked into another infirmary room when they'd arrived, and Harris hadn't seen her since. It was a relief to see her walking and looking relatively unscathed.

"I'm fine. They didn't hurt me."

"I'm sorry you had to go through all this," he said.

She hesitated at the end of his bed, so he patted the space next to his hip. "It's fine to come sit if you want."

She climbed up on the bed and folded her hands in her lap, staring at them. "It's my fault you were hurt."

Harris rested a hand on top of hers, squeezing them. "No. It was the fae's fault, and they're being dealt with."

He never touched patients, but this was different. Besides, there was no way he could be her therapist anymore. He'd have to transfer her to Kenya or Nick. They were too close after this shared trauma, and he wouldn't be able to be neutral and help her work through it.

Her face crumpled, and she turned and buried her head in his shoulder as the tears flowed. It was an awkward position, but he curved an arm around her and rubbed her back.

"You're safe now. The Tribunal is working with the Fae Council, and Jackson said we've both been cleared of all charges."

"What about the other guy? They killed him!"

It was exactly what Richard deserved, but Harris didn't think telling her that would help. Most Weres never witnessed how vicious retribution was when someone put the safety of the supernatural community at risk. It was a hard lesson to learn so young.

"He broke the law, Candice," Harris said gently. "He'd signed his own death sentence, whether it was by the hands of the fae or the Tribunal."

Harris was grateful that she'd been in the cell next to him so she didn't see them stab him. No doubt that would have been traumatizing. It wasn't going to go down as one of his fonder memories.

The sight of Jackson kneeling over him looking at him like he'd created the moon? That one was going to be saved for posterity.

A shadow fell over the doorway, and they looked up, tensed for trouble. It was just Drew, standing there with a clipboard and an exasperated expression.

"I told you to get some sleep, Harris," he scolded. "Candice, come with me. We need to get you dinner."

She eased away from Harris, ducking back in to give him a careful hug.

"Go. I'll see you tomorrow."

She nodded and left with Drew, who gave him a stern look before turning out the light and shutting the door.

Harris eased down on the pillows, trying to find a comfortable position. He let out a soft groan of pain when he jostled his head, and Jackson was at his side an instant later.

"I thought you were asleep," Harris said, smiling as Jackson rearranged pillows with singular focus.

"I was dozing. You're really good with her," Jackson said. "Just being near you made her heartbeat calm and her scent settle."

"It's my job."

Jackson pulled the fleece blanket higher, taking care as he tucked it around Harris's ribs. He leaned down and pressed a kiss to the tip of Harris's nose. "It's not just a job for you, Harry."

He settled into the place Candice had been sitting, curving his arm around Harris's head and leaning in close. "I can't ask you to leave Camp H.O.W.L. It's obvious how much you love helping these kids."

They hadn't talked about the reality of their mating and what it would mean for their careers. Harris braced himself. "I want to be wherever you are."

Jackson rested his forehead against Harris's. "Ditto. I'm going to talk to Anne Marie about a permanent position here as head of security. I think the last few weeks have proven you need one. It can't be a secondary task assigned to the staff anymore."

Harris's heart clenched. "No. Jackson, that's such a waste of your talent. You were made for bigger things. I can't ask you to give up all your dreams and stay here with me."

Jackson kissed his forehead and sat up so they were eye-to-eye. "I almost lost you, Harry. If we'd been a minute later, they'd have realized the spear didn't pierce your heart and come back to finish you off. You almost *died*. There's nothing more important than you. You're my mate."

Harris pushed him away and struggled to sit up with a wince. "No. I know the Enforcer job is out, but there are other careers out there. I'm not going to let you give up on being a Second. You were made for that position, Jackson."

Jackson pulled away. "So, I should walk away from you? Give you up right after I found you?"

Harris bunched the bedcovers in his fists. His mate was a stubborn son of a bitch. "No, Jackson. I'll go with you. I can work anywhere."

He held Jackson's gaze for a long, frustrating moment before breaking down and laughing. His head screamed, and he clutched at it, in pain but unable to stop his giggles.

"Our first big fight and it's about who is more willing to give up their career for the other," Harris said.

"Fuck that, our first fight was you walking away from me after the Tribunal called," Jackson said.

"Or maybe when you freaked out after you kissed me the first time," Harris said, his smile growing when Jackson gave him an affronted look.

"I should have known being mated to you would be a challenge," Jackson teased. He leaned in and gave Harris a soft kiss. "No running this time, see?"

Harris kissed him back, but his head protested, leaving him dizzy and sick.

"You're hurting yourself. You need to sleep. I'll be here in the morning."

Harris looked at him, wide-eyed. "You felt that through the bond?"

Jackson wrinkled his nose. "Yes."

That was amazing. Connecting during a time of extreme stress was one thing, but being able to sense his feelings right now was something else.

Harris closed his eyes and focused on the way the bond hummed through him, warm and comforting. He followed the thread of it, losing his concentration when he felt Jackson's concern and grudging amusement.

"I'm fine," he said, opening his eyes again.

"You'll be even more fine tomorrow. Drew said if you got some decent sleep, your body will heal the concussion overnight. No more stalling. Sleep."

He retucked Harris and then climbed onto the bed and stretched out in the narrow space beside him.

Harris luxuriated in the warmth of Jackson's body beside him, his wolf relaxing and sleepiness setting in. He turned his head toward Jackson, drifting off to the warm press of lips against his forehead.

"I'M just saying, give yourself some time before you make any major decisions."

Harris scowled at Tate's image on the screen, and Tate shrugged. "It's what you'd tell your own patients, and you know it."

He was right. After a traumatic experience, he'd tell his patients to put off big decisions for a while. Like quitting Camp H.O.W.L. without having a job to jump to.

He had his letter of resignation on his desk, printed and signed. He'd stay until Jackson landed somewhere, but he had no idea how long that would be.

"Have you thought about what we've been planning?"

Harris cracked a smile. "Oh, I see. The life-altering decision ban doesn't count if it benefits you?"

Tate chuckled. "Well, it's not out of left field. We've been talking about this since I set up my practice out here, and when Jackson was headed to the East Coast Tribunal Enforcers, you put a timeline of a year on it. I'm still good with that, but if you wanted to jump now, well, there's space for you. I've been turning clients away, which I hate to do. There's a huge need out here, man."

Harris had planned to buy into Tate's practice in New York, but mating with Jackson might take that off the table.

"I don't know if he'll want to be in New York City," Harris said, picking up a paper clip and playing with it. "Maybe he could get on the police force out there."

"Or he could move Fang and Fury here," Tate said. "There are a few established firms out this way, but there's plenty of work."

Harris shook his head. "Jordan is moving back to St. Louis and taking Fang and Fury with him. He'll operate out of there."

Moving to St. Louis was an option, but Jackson seemed lukewarm to the idea when Jordan brought it up over breakfast. He wanted to strike out on his own, and Harris could appreciate that.

"I'll talk to him about it," Harris said. "But like I told Jackson this morning, I'll go wherever he goes."

"You sound like a lovesick fool," Tate said, wrinkling his nose.

"I sound like you and Adrian circa a few years ago," Harris pointed out. "The two of you had this exact argument after he left Camp H.O.W.L. and went back to Portland. You wanted to move out there, and he didn't want you to give up your career here."

Tate flipped the camera off. "Whatever."

"You're the worst therapist," Harris laughed. "Maybe I don't want to go into a practice with you. Do you flip all your patients off?"

"Only the ones who are being idiots," Tate said. He paused and cocked his head. "My next appointment is here. Listen, why don't you two come to New York for a few days? I can show you the practice, and I'll find someone from the Pack to give Jackson a tour. I bet Alpha Connoll has connections that could help Jackson find a job."

Harris said his goodbyes and cut the connection. He put his letter of resignation in the desk drawer. Anne Marie wouldn't accept it from him right now anyway. He was on mandatory leave as of this morning. Two weeks. She told him she didn't care if he spent it at camp or somewhere else, but he wasn't going to be assigned any duties, and all of his patients had been divided up between Kenya and Nick.

Candice had taken the news hard, but he'd explained that he couldn't continue to see her as her therapist. As a friend, yes. He'd promised her she could call him day or night to talk about anything.

He scented Jackson a second before there were two quick knocks on his office door.

"Come in," he called, spinning in his chair to watch Jackson walk through the door. The sight of him took Harris's breath away. He couldn't believe Jackson was his. After all this time, his mate was his to touch and hold and order around.

"Take those boots off before you track mud all over my rug," he said.

"Nag, nag, nag," Jackson teased as he toed the boots off. "Just did a perimeter check, and everything's fine. The district Enforcer agreed to drop by once a week or so and do a patrol, but I think the camp's problems are over. Did you see Candice made a statement?"

He hadn't, but she'd talked to him about it this morning. Her agent had been sitting on a script about a girl in juvenile detention who learns the government is rounding up kids to force their parents to work for a secret agency, so she leads a revolution. They announced she'd been at Camp H.O.W.L. doing research on juvenile detention centers. The Tribunal signed off on it.

"We had a few paparazzi at the gates, but the park rangers ran them off. I think we're through the worst of it."

That was a relief. He didn't like that Camp H.O.W.L. was on the map at all, but this was the best resolution they could hope for. Part of him wished he could resurrect Richard so the Tribunal could kill him again. Most of this was that rat bastard's fault.

Harris reached his arms out, and Jackson straddled him in the chair. He nuzzled against Harris's neck. "Hey."

"Hey," Harris answered, his entire body settling as the warm weight of his mate caged him in. "Tate invited us to come out to New York. Meet the Pack. Maybe job hunt. What do you think?"

A knock interrupted them, and Harris groaned. Privacy hadn't been a thing they'd experienced yet as mates. It was frustrating.

Jackson nipped at his jaw before standing up. "I think that sounds wonderful, assuming we're getting a hotel room where we can be alone."

"Definitely," Harris muttered.

"Come in," Jackson said when the person knocked again.

Nick opened the door, his eyes averted like he was expecting them to be naked.

"For fuck's sake. Just come in," Harris groaned.

Nick laughed and shut the door behind him. He sank onto the couch. "I'm just dropping by to make sure you're not working. And to tell you that Anne Marie has been talking to a friend of Kenya's about filling in for you. She was one of Kenya's psychology students, and she's looking for work. Anne Marie offered her a temporary contract with the option to be brought on permanently if something opened up."

He gave Harris a significant look, and Harris sheepishly pulled his letter of resignation out of the desk and walked it over to give to Nick.

"That's what we thought. We didn't want to pressure you in case we were wrong, but it's pretty clear you two aren't going to be happy here."

"You heard us last night?" Harris felt stupid—they'd argued in the infirmary, and Nick lived upstairs. He probably heard every word.

"I wasn't trying to eavesdrop, but you two weren't quiet. I didn't say anything to Anne Marie, but you know she's got a freaky second sense for this kind of thing. She knew Tate was leaving before he knew himself, remember?"

She had. Anne Marie took her job as director seriously. She was their de facto Alpha, and she made their business her business. It was irritating at times, but it really did make the staff feel like a family. A Pack.

Jackson wrapped Harris in a hug from behind, resting his chin against Harris's shoulder. "I guess we'd better book those tickets to New York, then, huh?"

Chapter Sixteen

JACKSON left Harris happily geeking out over Tate's offices. Well, they were about to be *their* offices. He could tell from the excitement on his mate's face that Harris wanted to say yes to the offer. Jackson wasn't going to stand in the way of that, especially since New York City would have a lot of opportunities for him.

There were a few supernatural protection agencies he could work for, or he could stay in law enforcement. Either way, he'd be doing something he loved, and he'd be with Harris. Win-win.

A Were about his age named Stephen picked him up from Tate's offices to give him a tour of the city. It was a nice gesture from the local Alpha. Jackson was anxious to meet with the Pack, since if they moved here they'd be joining it. Harris had already met the Alpha,

since his children had attended Camp H.O.W.L. for
their Turns.

"The Pack compound in the city is actually an
apartment building," Stephen said, easing the car into
an alley that led to a parking garage. He opened the
grate with a fob and drove in. "Alpha Connoll has the
penthouse, and a good number of the Pack live here.
We have a few empty apartments, so if you and your
mate join us, you'd be invited to rent here."

An entire apartment building full of Weres? "There
aren't any humans here?"

"No. The Pack owns the building and operates it
as a private co-op. Apartments never go on the open
market. Pack allies are also welcome to live here, so
you'll see other shifters and a few nymphs. We have
alliances with all of the local supernatural groups."

It was so different from St. Louis. The Pack there
was large, but they all had their own homes spread out
across the city. The Pack compound was on the outskirts
of the city, where there was room to have acres of land
the Pack could run.

"How do you handle full moons?"

Stephen parked the car and led Jackson to an elevator.
"We have land outside the city. It's about an hour's drive.
There's a Pack house there, but most of us camp unless it's
really cold. We don't get much nature, so the time we do
spend out there we tend to go all wolf and stay outside."

It made sense. Jackson had lived in Lexington
long enough to appreciate the freedom he'd grown up
with living in the Pack house in St. Louis. He couldn't
imagine spending the year after his Turn worrying
about exposing the werewolf secret if he wolfed out at
home in the yard.

"We've converted the basement to a place we can shift and play," Stephen explained. He hit the penthouse button. "There are obstacles to climb and a lot of greenery. Alpha Connoll installed growing lights down there so we can have real plants, and everyone jokes that the Pack is going to get busted for growing pot because of them." He looked at Jackson nervously. "We don't, of course. Alpha Connoll told me you're a police officer."

"A drug enforcement officer, actually," he said, chuckling when Stephen paled. "But don't worry. We'd need a lot more red flags than ordering growing lights before you merited a raid. You're safe."

Stephen nodded, blowing out a breath. "We have a few Pack members in law enforcement. They keep an ear to the ground."

"And help cover up things too," Jackson said, nodding in approval. "A Pack your size should have people integrated at every level of city government."

"One of the Alpha's sons works in the mayor's office," Stephen said, his pride in his Pack showing in his tone. "And Adrian—you know him, I think? He's in the city planner's office now. We also have a Pack member who's a social worker. He keeps an eye out for supernatural kids who might have been funneled into the foster system."

It was impressive. The Pack took its role seriously in the city, protecting the supernatural residents as well as its own members. And if a few of the Pack were already in law enforcement, maybe they could help him get a job.

"Alpha Connoll wanted to meet with you. When you two are done, I can show you around the building."

Jackson swallowed his surprise, trying to look nonchalant.

"That would be great," Jackson said.

When it became clear Stephen wasn't going to step off the elevator with him, Jackson reached out to shake his hand. Stephen tilted his head and cast his eyes down, a traditional sign of deference for a higher-ranking Pack member. It was strange, but it felt right. Jackson thought about all the times he'd seen someone do this for his father. He reached out and lightly scented Stephen, his wrist grazing Stephen's neck. He wondered if all the Pack members were so deferential, or if it was specific to Stephen. Stephen shouldn't be averting his eyes to a visitor—he had to have a decent place in the Pack if the Alpha trusted him to speak on its behalf.

Jackson stepped out into an opulent hallway. Between the marble floor and the deep cherry wainscoting, it looked like an expensive hotel, not someone's personal apartment. He crossed the small lobby in three steps and rang the bell next to the only door he could see.

Jackson stepped back when the Alpha himself opened it. He was a big man with silvering hair and laugh lines. Jackson liked him immediately. He radiated authority but also kindness.

Jackson tilted his head, averting his eyes in the traditional greeting for someone of higher rank. The Alpha rumbled out a laugh and ran a wrist across the skin, then clapped him on the back.

"You were raised right, kiddo," he said, stepping back and inviting Jackson in. "Your dad is the Second for the Garrison Pack, right? I've met him a few times. Nice guy. Brutally efficient when he needs to be."

It was a high compliment coming from an Alpha. As the Pack Second, all the dirty work fell to his dad. He was in charge of solving problems—no questions asked. Jackson had wanted to be exactly like him for as long as he could remember.

"Thank you, Alpha Connoll. I am honored to be here. Thank you for your kind invitation. Stephen has been quite the tour guide."

Alpha Connoll laughed. "Laid it on thick, did he? This is his first time as a Pack liaison, and he's itching to show me he's big enough for the britches."

"He's done you proud, sir."

"I'm sure he has. He's been in training for over a year. Our current liaison is retiring in the spring, and Stephen is being groomed as her replacement. He's her son, so there's a lot of pressure on him to do well."

Alpha Connoll led Jackson over to a small bar and offered him a drink, which Jackson declined. It was just the two of them, and he couldn't let the Alpha serve him. It was basic Were etiquette, and he couldn't afford any missteps if he hoped to have a place in the Pack.

The Alpha nodded approvingly, moving them over to the couch. Jackson waited until the Alpha settled in a recliner before he took his seat. It earned him another smile, and he couldn't help but think this meeting was a series of tests to feel out Jackson's worthiness. He was determined to pass them.

"I don't usually meet with prospective Pack members this early," Alpha Connoll said, giving Jackson an assessing look. "But you knew that."

It was extremely rare for an Alpha to meet with a Were bidding to join their Pack this early in the process. Jackson had expected to meet with the Pack liaison, and if that went well, the Second, before meeting with Alpha Connoll.

"My Second's daughter is marrying into a Pack in Pennsylvania," Alpha Connoll said. "He petitioned to go with her. She's all the family he has, and he wants to be close to her and her pups. I don't have anyone internally that's a good choice for his replacement."

Normally in a Pack this size, the Second would have a Second of his own, someone who was being trained to take over. It was odd that the Connoll Pack didn't.

"My daughter had been training for the position, but she and the Alpha-in-Training aren't a good fit. I love my kids, but they are enough to try the patience of Job. I thought they'd grow out of this antagonism, but they haven't." He held a hand up like he expected Jackson to interject, which he would never do. "They're in their thirties. If it's not better by now, it's not going to get better. So we need to look externally for a Second. I've been watching your career, son. I'm impressed. And when you found your mate and torched your career for him? I was cheering on the sidelines."

Alpha Connoll must have been the second Alpha on the Tribunal who supported sending the Enforcers in to rescue Harris and Candice.

"Sir, I wouldn't say I torched my career. I still have a deep commitment to working in law enforcement and Pack politics. I—"

The Alpha waved away his protest. "Son, it was a compliment. You walked away from something you've been training to do for your entire life—something most Weres consider the highest honor in Pack politics—for love. That takes guts. And it shows how much you value your word. To borrow a phrase from my youngest, coming into the Tribunal and looking us in the eye and turning that job down was badass."

Jackson flushed and looked away. He'd assumed the Tribunal Alphas thought he was weak after he'd turned the job down. It was nice to hear at least one of them didn't.

"The way you were able to put your personal feelings aside and run a rescue mission shows me you've got an iron will too."

"Oh, sir. I didn't run that mission. Enforcer Abernathy did."

Alpha Connoll's laugh filled the room. "Trust me, I read the report. You had a significant role in it. Abernathy was beyond impressed with you. In fact, she even petitioned the Tribunal to see if we would make an exception to the bond rule for you."

Jackson's heart leaped.

"Unfortunately, we can't. It's there for a good reason. As you well know." The Alpha reached out and pushed a thick file folder across the table. "These are the details of the Connoll Pack. Number of members, Pack affiliations, all the treaties we've signed in the last twenty years. The alliances we're duty bound to uphold. The threats we face. Take some time, look it over. Stephen will set you up in an empty apartment on the floor below this one. Get to know my Pack, and if you like what you see, you can come on the next full-moon run with us."

Jackson took the folder. He felt like he was a beat behind. "Sir?"

Alpha Connoll stood, and Jackson followed on autopilot. The Alpha put a hand on Jackson's shoulder and squeezed it. "I think you'd be an outstanding Second for this Pack. You have a good head on your shoulders, and you're obviously good at what you do. Your work with Fang and Fury puts you in a position to be able to handle electronic surveillance and security for the Pack, which is something we've had to outsource until now. Read through that. Talk it over with your mate. And if you two are up for it, we'll give it a test run at the full moon. If you can get along with my hard-headed son and the rest of the Pack, the job is yours."

Jackson was speechless. Alpha Connoll had turned his world upside down. He'd resigned himself to never achieving his goal, and now it was being handed to him on a silver platter.

Jackson followed the Alpha to the door, relieved to see Stephen standing there when it opened. Stephen was beaming at him, grinning ear-to-ear when he saw the thick file. "It went well, then. Awesome!"

The Alpha laughed. "Get him some lunch, Stephen. Kid's going to go into shock if you don't get some sugar into him."

Jackson grimaced. He'd been so overwhelmed that he'd forgotten his manners.

"I apologize, Alpha Connoll," he said, tilting his head again. "Thank you for this generous offer. I look forward to getting to know your Pack."

The Alpha didn't seem big on propriety because he brushed the apology off. "Don't worry about it. This is a lot, and I ambushed you. Take as much time as you need. If you have any questions, let Stephen know, and he can get you the answers. Most of the Pack will be leaving for the cabin tomorrow at noon. We like to spend a few days out there before the moon when it's possible. Both you and your mate are welcome to run with us, and there will be a room for you at the Pack house. Stephen can arrange transportation for you."

Jackson couldn't do much more than nod. Stephen took pity on him and guided him into the elevator with a wink. He took him down a floor and used a set of keys to let him into one of the apartments.

"There are two on this floor. Our current Second is in the other one, but this one is empty at the moment. There's a private stairwell up to the Alpha's quarters, so it's reserved for family or Seconds."

It wasn't furnished, but it had soapstone countertops and wood floors that were the same burnished color as the wainscoting in the hallway. The walls were all painted white, and there were a few gigantic windows looking out over the city. The kitchen and sitting room blended together into one big space, with two hallways leading off it.

"Three bedrooms down here," Stephen said, waving toward one hallway, "and a study and library this way. The study opens into the master suite, which is also down that hallway."

Jackson was floored by how open the space was. The ceilings must have been nine or ten feet. It didn't feel like stuffy apartment. It felt like a space a Were could be comfortable in. "Are all the apartments this big?"

"They all have the high ceilings, but most aren't quite as large as this. There are only two apartments on this floor. Most of the floors have four to six apartments. We also have an entire floor in the middle dedicated to a nursery school and play space."

This was amazing. Jackson put his file folder on the counter and pulled up a stool. He was trying hard not to get attached, but he could already picture Harris cooking at the gas range in the corner.

"I'll leave you to look through that. What would you like for lunch?"

Jackson shrugged. "Whatever's easy."

Stephen rolled his eyes, then seemed to realize that wasn't becoming of a Pack liaison. "Sorry. I'll pick up an assortment of sandwiches. Would you like me to have your mate brought here when he's done with Dr. Lewis?"

Jackson had already started in on the paperwork. "Please," he said, turning another page. Even the Pack financials were here. Alpha Connoll must be dead serious about his offer if he was giving Jackson this kind of insight without a commitment from him. Then again, he'd be crazy to turn this offer down. The Alpha had to know that.

He glanced at his phone after Stephen let himself out, wondering if he should text Harris. This was big news and his first instinct was to share it with his mate.

Signing the paperwork with Tate yet?

A second later his phone dinged.

You know I wouldn't without talking to you. But he may or may not be having a lawyer draw them up.

Jackson grinned. This was perfect. They could both be happy here without giving anything up.

I might have a job offer.

Harris responded with a key smash of characters, most of them exclamation points.

I'm not surprised. You're amazing.

Jackson grinned. He'd wait to drop exactly what the offer was on Harris until they were together. He wanted to see his mate's face when he told him that being mated to him had helped all his dreams come true.

Chapter Seventeen

Three months later

JACKSON tugged at his sweaty T-shirt, pulling it over his head the moment he entered his apartment. The last time he'd led a sparring class shirtless, two girls and the Alpha's youngest son Ryan ended up knocked on their asses and injured, so he'd adopted a strict no-nudity policy in the gym.

The Pack had balked when he'd suggested classes on how to fight, but once they'd realized how much fun it was, there had been a surge of interest.

Harris said it was because the teacher was hot, but Jackson thought he was biased. The shirtlessness incident backed that theory up, which was why he now taught in a loose Camp H.O.W.L. T-shirt of Harris's and basketball shorts.

"Honey, I'm home," he called out. He tossed his T-shirt on the counter, doubling back when he thought about how angry Harris would be. He detoured into the laundry room instead, dutifully putting it in a pile of dirty clothes.

Their apartment was gorgeous, and letting it get cluttered would be a crime. Plus, as Second, their door was always open. Figuratively. He'd made the mistake of leaving it unlocked once, and he and Harris would probably never live it down.

Jackson heard voices in the study and made his way there. Harris was skyping Candice. Her latest movie premiere was next week in New York, and Harris was going with her.

Jackson peeked around the doorframe, his mouth going dry when he saw Harris had been modeling the tuxedo Candice's agent sent over for him. Jackson whistled, making Candice laugh and Harris blush.

"Looks like you've got a half-naked mate who wants your attention," she teased. "Hi, Jackson!"

Jackson grinned and slid into the chair Harris had vacated so he could see the screen. "Hey, Candice. We still on for ramen when you're here?"

"Yes, God. Emma's coming too, if that's okay. They haven't been letting me eat *anything* because they're afraid I'm not going to be able to fit into the dress Dior is lending me for the premiere. I've been eating protein bars in the bathroom to get enough calories."

Jackson laughed. "I keep telling you we need to find you a supernatural agent."

She rolled her eyes. "I know."

"We'll do some looking when you're here," he said. He pressed a sloppy kiss to Harris's cheek and sauntered out of the room, giving him a heated look where he knew the camera wouldn't catch it.

"Gotta go," Harris said. Jackson could feel his eyes on him, so he swept his basketball shorts and boxers off, adding a swagger to his hips as he walked into their bedroom. "See you next week, sweetie. You're still staying here?"

"Is it safe?"

Jackson laughed at the open judgment and horror in Candice's tone.

"Mostly," Harris said. "And the guest room is at the other end of the apartment, so…."

Candice's tinkling laugh rang through the wall. "Okay. I guess if I see anything that traumatizes me, I know a good psychologist."

Harris laughed and closed the laptop with a snap.

"Don't take that off!" Jackson yelled from the bedroom.

Harris was laughing when he appeared in the hallway. His bow tie was untied and the first few buttons were undone.

"Tuxedo does it for you, huh?"

"Baby, on you? A ratty old bathrobe would do it for me. But I want to savor this. I need to build up an immunity so I don't jump you in front of Candice."

"She'd never forgive you. Remember how angry Ryan was when the elevator opened and we were making out?"

The Alpha's son had ranted about how he was going to have to take the stairs because the elevator was going to reek for days. He'd been smiling when he said it, so Jackson wasn't too worried about emotionally scarring him, but he did worry he and Harris might be starring in his fantasies for a while.

Which was fine, as long as the kid realized Harris was his. Not that there was much doubt. The two of them completed their bonding ceremony two months ago, combining it with the ceremony that officially adopted them into the Pack. They'd held off on his formal Second installation until earlier this month, even though he'd been Acting Second since they moved in. Alpha Connoll had suggested it, and Jackson was forever in his debt. He'd been feeling pretty antisocial after the bonding ceremony—he didn't think he'd have been able to go through the rest of the rituals without throwing Harris over his shoulder and running out.

The bond was settling, though it was still touchy. Tate said that was normal. It would be a few months before either of them could take a trip or be apart for more than a night, but that was okay. Jackson didn't foresee wanting to be apart from Harris for a good long time.

Jackson watched as Harris slowly undressed. He loved this private side of his mate. He was playful and so full of joy.

Jackson was practically panting by the time Harris was naked. How could he want him this much? The need was just as overwhelming as it had been the first time. He was constantly hungry for the feeling of his mate's skin against him. It was a good thing that Harris didn't work in the building, or they'd never get anything done.

Harris climbed up the mattress until he was straddling Jackson, their naked thighs touching. Even that was almost too much, thanks to the feedback loop through the bond. He'd thought it was intense their first time, but he'd been wrong. He couldn't even put into words what it felt like to experience his mate's pleasure along with his own.

Harris leaned down and kissed his chest, humming happily. "Come in from the gym?"

Jackson arched when he moved up to his neck, kissing and sucking at the tender skin. "Yes. I had a class."

"Mmm. I like when you're all sweaty."

Jackson knew. Sometimes he went for a run shortly before Harris was due to come home exactly for this reason.

Harris kissed him and brought their hips together, rutting against Jackson. Pleasure sparked through him, white-hot but far from enough. Jackson wrapped his hands around Harris's waist and flipped them so he could kiss his way down his body, paying special attention to his bobbing cock. When Harris started to squirm, he delved deeper, licking over his entrance and drinking up his mate's cries.

One of the many benefits of the bond was being able to tell when Harris was getting close. The way Harris pushed a bottle of lube into his hands was also a good tell. Jackson eased away, grinning at Harris's needy groan, and lubed himself up, replacing his tongue with his cock. The delicious slide inside always made his vision gray, and Jackson stopped when he'd bottomed out. Once they'd recovered from the bond flaring, he set a steady pace, knowing exactly how Harris liked it. They didn't have much time, so he couldn't take him apart until he was crying, but he'd do that later. They had so much sex these days even Jackson's teenage self was impressed.

He could feel Harris's orgasm building along with his own, so he leaned in and cradled Harris's head as he drove into him, breathing in his scent. Jackson still couldn't believe he got to have this every day. He couldn't imagine a better life.

His orgasm took him by surprise, and he sped up his strokes, determined to take Harris over with him. It didn't take much for him to follow, both of them gasping and arching together.

Jackson stilled, enjoying listening to Harris's pulse race. He pressed a kiss against his neck and eased out of him, rolling to the side so he didn't crush him. Harris stretched and grabbed a pack of wet wipes in the headboard, cleaning them up quickly. They kept supplies in nearly every room in the apartment, earning them eye rolls and sighs every time someone opened a drawer looking for a pen and pulled out wet wipes or lube.

Jackson refused to be embarrassed by it. He had a healthy appetite for his mate, and as far as he was concerned, they had ten years to make up for. He didn't know why his wolf waited so long to fall in love with Harris, but he was glad it had.

New York was a big lifestyle change for them, but they were finding there was a diverse supernatural community surrounding them. It was eye-opening, seeing how much good Harris was doing with his practice, counseling supernaturals of all backgrounds. And Jackson had never been as fulfilled as he was acting as Second for the Connoll Pack. Every day brought new challenges and new experiences.

And he got to go through them all with Harris at his side.

His mate had been hiding in plain sight for all of their adult lives, and he was grateful every day that he'd found him.

Author's Note

AS the Camp H.O.W.L. series comes to a close I wanted to talk about the Hoosier National Forest, which is the perfect place to hide a werewolf camp. Southern Indiana has several large, heavily forested parks. And speaking as someone who's lived there--let's just say the wolves wouldn't be the weirdest people around.

The Hoosier National Forest is a great place to lose yourself in nature for an afternoon or a weekend (or a month of how-to-werewolf classes). National parks are under threat from both climate change and political posturing, and they need an advocate. That's why I'm donating a portion of the royalties from the Camp H.O.W.L. series to the National Parks Conservation Association. We need to preserve these parks for future generations--and werewolves, of course.

I hope you've enjoyed visiting Camp H.O.W.L. as much as I have. And don't worry, you'll see familiar faces in my next project, the Connoll Pack series. Look for that in early 2019, starting with *Stealing His Heart*.

As always, thanks for reading!

Bru

Now Available

REAMSPUN BEYOND

Under a Blue Moon

By Bru Baker
A Camp H.O.W.L. Novel

Once in a blue moon, opposites find they're a perfect match.

Nick Perry is tired of helping people with their marriages, so when a spot opens up to work with teens at Camp H.O.W.L., he jumps at it. He doesn't expect to fall in lust with the dreamy new camp doctor, Drew Welch. But Drew is human, and Nick has seen secrets ruin too many relationships to think that a human/werewolf romance can go anywhere.

Happy-go-lucky Drew may not sprout claws, but he's been part of the Were community all his life. He has no trouble fitting in at the camp—except for Nick's stubborn refusal to acknowledge the growing attraction between them and his ridiculous stance on dating humans. Fate intervenes when one of his private practice patients threatens Drew's life. Will the close call help Nick to see a connection like theirs isn't something to let go of?

Now Available at
www.dreamspinnerpress.com

Coming in October 2018

⟲REAMSPUN BEYOND

Dreamspun Beyond #29
The Librarian's Ghost by Sean Michael

Can love survive the perils of MacGregor House?

The Supernatural Explorers are back and looking for their next big paranormal case. They might've found it in a plea from Payne, a mild-mannered librarian who has inherited the family mansion—MacGregor House. Since moving in a few months ago, Payne's exhausted the list of ghost hunters and experts in his quest for help. The Supers are his last chance.

So why does normally good-natured cameraman Will take an instant dislike to Payne? For that matter, why has he felt irritable and angry since they arrived at the site? It soon becomes clear that the answers they seek will be found in the basement—where nobody has gone since Payne was a little boy. As the haunting grows deadlier, things get sweeter between Will and Payne, but all hell's about to break loose when they breach the basement door.

Will they be ready?

Dreamspun Beyond #30
Calculated Magic by SJD Peterson

Never too late for love.

Three-hundred-and-fifty-year-old warlock Tikron must find his true love or forfeit his immortality. But if he hasn't found his ideal mate in all these centuries, the prospect don't look too bright.

That is, until he sees mathematician Richard Beaumont. It's love at first sight and Tikron's future just got a whole lot brighter.

Except Richard doesn't believe in love at first sight. He doesn't believe in love at all. He certainly doesn't believe in magic. His life is ruled by statistics and logic, and they tell him a relationship with Tikron has only a 10 percent chance of success. That's unacceptable—even if the attraction between them is off the charts.

With his powers waning and the clock ticking down, Tikron's last hope is showing Richard the true meaning of magic.